CRASH
DIVE

John Townsend

Megan

Don't have nightmares!

John Townsend

Acorn Independent Press

ISBN 978-1-908318-86-2

This is a work of fiction. All characters, organisations, situations and events portrayed in this novel are from the author's imagination and have been depicted entirely fictitiously.

www.acornindependentpress.com

ABOUT THE AUTHOR

John Townsend writes a wide range of children's books for all ages, from fiction and plays to non-fiction and reading schemes for schools. He can often be found in classrooms trying to enthuse young people about literacy, books and the exciting power of stories.

PRAISE FOR CRASH DIVE

"John Townsend is skilled at maintaining the tension in Crash Dive... a pacy, upbeat adventure story... an engaging book... among this summer's best young adult fiction."

The Independent on Sunday

"Great fun; a real page-turner. Barney's the sort of character many young teenage readers could relate to: lively, funny, clever and, like many teenagers, misunderstood!"

National Literacy Association

***"Don't read this book if you suffer from vertigo.** Crash Dive is well-written, never dull and held my attention to the end. Barney is an engaging character... there is plenty here to engage teenage readers."*

**The School Librarian
(School Library Association)**

OTHER ADVENTURE FICTION BY JOHN TOWNSEND

Shorter Barney Stories:
Deadline
ISBN 9781842994610
Barrington Stoke

Firebomb
ISBN 9781842995198
Barrington Stoke

Icefall
ISBN 9781842995709
Barrington Stoke

Stage play:
Ski Jump
ISBN 9780435075422
Pearson

www.johntownsend.co.uk

Chapter 1

Hidden eyes were watching. Staring.

Barney slammed the car door, slung his sports bag over his shoulder and raised his arm. The silver Mazda pulled away into a stream of airport traffic as a hand waving back from the driver's window slipped inside to grip the steering wheel.

"Bye, Mum," he called after her, before turning to squint up into the clouds above the control tower where a passenger jet was roaring heavenwards, seeming to hang momentarily in the darkening sky. He reached into a pocket for his airline ticket marked 'unaccompanied minor – aged 13', checked his watch yet again and hurried towards the automatic glass doors beneath those familiar chrome letters: DEPARTURES.

Striding across the vast shiny floor, Barney gazed up to check the departures board. He felt he was taking a lot in his stride lately, especially this fortnightly flight to Scotland to spend the weekend with his dad. But, being August, his usual flight was full so he was flying later than normal. Not that anything seemed much different – or so he thought.

The eyes were watching him from the top of the escalator – far enough away to remain unnoticed.

Barney didn't see the staring figure in dark glasses, with a gloved hand holding a phone… zooming in to record his every move. A clear image of his face was being beamed far away. The signal was transmitted secretly and silently to a satellite somewhere beyond the clouds, up there in the ever-darkening sky, where he would soon be speeding through the darkness himself, heading northwards into the looming night.

Chapter 2

The black sky flashed and crackled with shuddering explosions of swirling colour. Crimson smoke drifted over the castle ramparts and shimmering rooftops until a final spray of splintering silver burst over the city in a blinding blaze.

"To bigger fireworks this time next year!" The woman on the balcony sipped a spritzer and raised her glass. The dying sparks glinted in its dancing bubbles and in the pinhead of rose quartz in her eyebrow ring.

"To this time next year," the man's oily voice repeated. "When it will all be very different. Fireworks in every sense." His sinister snigger cut a chill through the balmy August night as he lit a cigarette, rested an elbow on the rail and peered down into the street.

"But there's plenty of work to be done first." He sighed.

"Like recruits," the woman added with an edge of urgency, taking another sip and smearing her glass with purple lipstick. "To do the dirty work and act as a decoy."

"I'll sort that out," he snapped.

She shrugged. "I still think a kid's a good idea. Someone to fetch and carry but who won't have a clue. And after all, who'd suspect a schoolboy?"

"I hate kids." He blew smoke into the night and brushed ash from his sleeve as he grunted, "They're all bolshie brats these days. Too full of themselves. Full of attitude."

The woman laughed. "And you're not? Just leave it to me, Geoff. I'll find someone. Someone young – like a lamb to the slaughter. A kid travelling alone would be best. Someone who can easily be fooled and won't be missed… when it's time to kill him."

She reached into her leopard-print handbag and smiled at the image which had just arrived on her phone. "It seems as if we might already have a candidate. Our lookout has found a kid at the airport. He looks as though butter wouldn't melt in his pretty little mouth. Perfect."

Barney's face looked up at her from her phone screen, reflecting a swirl of colours from the last firework fizzing above her head. She said nothing as her fingers tapped the keys.

"No kid is perfect," the man murmured. "Boys are the worst."

"Trust me – this one will be ideal." She pressed 'send'. "I'm an excellent judge of character. He's got wide, innocent eyes. He'll be putty in our hands."

Her text arrived at the airport in seconds – short and simple: **GET HIM**.

Chapter 3

The eyes were still watching... getting closer.

A tall woman in dark glasses under a mop of frizzy black hair tapped her white plastic stick around Barney's feet as he sat absorbed in his book in the departure lounge.

"Can I sit here?" she asked.

"Sure," he said. "Do you need a hand?"

"I can manage, thank you. You sound quite young – are you by yourself?"

"Yeah," he said, somewhat puzzled.

He watched her sit down opposite him and wondered how much she could really see. Her eyes were totally hidden behind the sunglasses and her voice sounded foreign when she whispered, "Travelling alone, are you? That's very brave."

"I do it all the time. It's only to Glasgow. Nowhere very scary."

"You don't know Glasgow." She laughed.

"I know it quite well, actually. I go there a lot and I like it," he said, looking over his shoulder at the door marked 'STAFF ONLY', before checking his watch. It wouldn't be long before a steward would come to collect him.

"You seem a bit on edge," she said. "Don't you like flying?"

"I love it, actually. But the thing is, and I don't mean to be rude or anything, but why have you got dark glasses and a white stick when it seems like you can see OK?"

The woman shifted awkwardly, saying nothing. Eventually she smiled. "So how can you tell?"

"My gran's blind and she's got a guide dog. I'm used to all her quirky little ways. She never sits down without feeling the seat first to make sure it's safe. You just plonked straight down. Gran wears a special watch that speaks the time when she presses the buttons but yours is just normal. What's the good of a tiny watch face if you're blind? And my gran never wears gloves as she says her fingertips are her spare eyes. I bet you can't feel a thing even through those thin gloves. And the thing is, who wears gloves in August unless they want to hide something on their hands? So, am I right?"

"Well observed," she said uneasily. "You seem like a bright kid. Ideal. A good detective, too – judging by the book you're reading."

"I'm in to crime at the moment." Barney smiled. "I don't mean me personally. I might be a pain in the neck at times but I'm not a criminal. I just like CSI and mysteries and stuff. This book's a great story about a kidnap."

"Really?" The glasses hid the reaction in her eyes. She folded her stick and put it in her bag. "I reckon you're just the sort of lad I'm looking for. My company is on the lookout for bright young people like you."

"Maybe if you took off the shades you'd be able to look more easily," he said with a grin.

She neither smiled nor removed her glasses. "We'd pay well," she said curtly.

"That's very kind of you but the last thing Mum said to me as I got out of the car was 'stranger danger'. So I'm afraid I can't do deals with strange women in airports. Sorry. Mum would go ballistic. So if you'll excuse me, I'd better find my steward."

He stood and dropped his book in his bag, just as a blonde ponytailed woman in airline uniform emerged through the staff door.

"Hi, Barney – you've got me again. Great to see you. And I see I've also got the pleasure of your company in two weeks. You're booked on the seventeen fifty-three then. You're becoming my special little regular traveller, eh?"

"Yeah," he said, looking over his shoulder one last time at the strange frizzy-haired woman who was still sitting motionless, before the steward led him through the departure gate towards the awaiting plane.

Without removing her sunglasses, the woman took from her handbag a slim tartan-covered notebook and scribbled: *Barney. Friday, 2 weeks. 17.53 – Glasgow.*

Then she casually sent a text:

```
Nearly got him. Need back-up in
2 weeks. Then he's ours.
```

Chapter 4

The security officer stood with his arms folded across his wide chest, chewing gum and glaring. His eyes were fierce, staring from a mean face with a sweaty upper lip and blotchy double-chin. "Next. You, lad."

Barney stepped forward to put his sports bag on the conveyor belt, sensing the hostile glare and officious tone in the man's voice.

"On your own, son? Where are your parents?"

"I'm alone," Barney answered sheepishly. He wanted to say, " Actually, they're in my bag," but it wasn't worth the risk. His sports bag trundled along the conveyor belt towards the x-ray machine. "I'm going to Glasgow to stay with my dad. Mum's just dropped me off."

"Is that so?" the man muttered, showing no interest whatsoever. "Take off your trainers."

As Barney stooped to untie his laces, he saw an x-ray operator lifting his trampoline trophy. Barney grinned proudly. "That's my gym award. I'm taking it to show my dad."

"That's what you think, son." The security officer picked it up with a sneer and studied the engraved letters with a mocking edge to his voice. "'Barney Jones. Trampoline. Grade 3. Under 18. Full marks for Barani,

Straddle Jump and Crash Dive.' I hope you won't be doing any of that on the plane."

Trying to hide his irritation, Barney replied as politely as he could, "A crash dive is a trampolining term for a three-quarter front somersault. It's got nothing to do with an air disaster – unless I happen to trip going down the plane steps."

"Is that so?" The man chewed his gum vigorously, oblivious to Barney's attempt at a joke.

"So what's a barani? No Indian takeaways allowed on the flight."

"Actually, a barani is a front somersault with a half-twist."

"Of lemon?" The man smirked. He snorted, wheezing out his spearminty breath. "You're still not taking it on the flight. Take your belt off."

Barney's instinct was to argue but he knew it was pointless so he sighed audibly, unbuckled his belt and rolled it up beside his wallet and trainers in a tray. It instantly uncoiled and wriggled like a shot cobra. The officer stepped forward to frisk him.

"Arms out," he snapped, clearly enjoying his sense of power. Barney held his breath to avoid the smell of gum and stale sweat. As the man stooped to feel around Barney's ankles, his flabby stomach spilled over his own belt and Barney looked down to see tufty black hair around a bald patch with a purple birthmark like an upside-down Australia. It took all his willpower not to mention that Tasmania and the Great Barrier Reef were missing.

"You're not really going to confiscate my trampolining trophy, are you?" Barney asked, as politely as he could manage. "I really want my dad to see it so I can impress him for once."

"Tough. In the wrong hands, it could be a lethal weapon. Sharp corners and that little brass athlete poking his arm up could take someone's eye out if you slammed it in their face."

"But I'm hardly likely to, am I? Do I really look like a terrorist?"

The man spun round and brought his nose right up to Barney's. The minty breath couldn't disguise the smell of cigarettes. "And just tell me, son: what does a terrorist look like exactly? Please tell me, as it would make my job a hell of a lot easier. Now, collect your bag and wait over there to be collected by a steward."

"Will I be able to pick up my trophy when I come back?"

"I doubt it. I don't guarantee anything. Next."

Barney was about to say that, according to his last school report, it was supposed to be *him* with the attitude problem, but he managed to stop himself just in time. He remembered the card he'd written to himself after a disastrous parents' evening. 'Note to self: I must stop speaking my thoughts or making jokes – even if they're the best in the history of the universe. My mission is to upset no one and please everyone. Boring but safe.' So far he gave himself 7 out of 10 for effort.

"Hi, are you Barney by any chance?" A tall, slim woman in familiar sky-blue uniform with red neck scarf approached him with a beaming smile. She wore thick make-up, had a mass of peroxide blonde curls and enormous false eyelashes. As she shook his hand Barney felt the stickiness of fresh nail varnish and the wafting smell of pear drops.

"Yeah. Barney Jones. You're not my usual steward. Where's Patsy?"

"We changed shifts. She said to say 'Hi'. I'm Elaine and I'm your major for your journey."

"Major?"

"That's right. You're an unaccompanied minor so I'm your major who'll deliver you to your destination nice and happy. You look cute!"

Barney kept to his new rules and said nothing about her appearance – however much that he wanted to.

"If you'd like to come along with me, we'll see about a drink and a biscuit before we board. How's that?" She led him into a small room where the light from a flickering fluorescent tube blinked off of a plastic cup of orange squash and the foil of a Penguin biscuit, which were laid out on a table.

"You really shouldn't have gone to so much trouble." He smiled. "I've never had such first-class treatment before."

"It's a pleasure." His sarcasm was either missed or deliberately ignored. "So how come you're travelling on your own? It says here you're thirteen." She flicked through papers on her clipboard.

"Yeah. Mum and Dad are divorced and Dad lives in Glasgow, so I spend a lot of weekends with him. He says he can usually find a window for me at the weekend and I always say I hope I don't smash it! That's because I tend to annoy him – especially when we play golf."

Elaine took a sip of water, leaving her lipstick smeared on the white plastic cup.

"Golf sounds fun," she said with her fixed smile. "I bet your mum misses having you around, though."

"Yeah." His cup suddenly split and leaked orange down his sleeve. Elaine looked at her watch, still smiling as she hurriedly smoothed a sticking plaster across the back of her hand.

"We'll have to board in a few minutes." The time sparkled on her unusual bracelet-watch.

Barney was intrigued. "Wow, I thought my watch with a cow face and mooing alarm was really cool but I've never seen one like that before."

She beamed proudly. "Given to me by an admirer. Very exclusive – Seiko. I can display the time in any mode I choose and at anywhere in the world." She demonstrated by pressing buttons along the elegant black and silver bracelet. "The time shows up along this continuous sapphire crystal. I love it. But it tells me we need to make a move. Do you want a make sure before we go?"

"Sorry?"

"The loo. You can use the staff one next door if you like." She threw her cup at a litter bin but it bounced off the rim and wedged behind the fridge.

"Yeah – I need to wash this sticky orange off my hands." He left his bag with her and entered the door marked 'STAFF', before going down a corridor and into the men's washroom. He rinsed his hands, shook them under a drier that nearly blew off his fingers and was about to walk out when he felt the screwed up Penguin wrapper in his pocket. There was no litter bin so he went into one of the cubicles to flush it away, just as footsteps entered the washroom. The door of the next cubicle slammed against the partition as it was kicked forcefully. Then Barney's half-closed door was pushed open just as aggressively, knocking into him and squashing him behind it, out of sight.

The voice beside him was all-too-familiar. "It's OK, there's no one in here. I can talk."

Barney froze. It was the security officer – the one with Australia on his head. He was speaking into his phone just the other side of the cubicle door.

"Listen, the kid's alone with just hand luggage. I took a trophy thing off him – some sort of trampolining award. It might work so I say we give it a try. Nothing to lose."

Barney held his breath, desperate not to move. But what if his trainers showed under the door? He tried to slide them sideways but the soles squeaked on the tiles. The man continued speaking, sounding more distant now, as if he'd turned away.

"I don't like him. He's a cocky little devil. You know I don't think a kid's a good idea. I hate them. Jan says this one's got something about him but I beg to differ. His flight to Glasgow leaves soon so I'll have to rush. I'll let you know how it goes this end and be prepared for putting the plan into operation."

Unable to hold his breath any longer, Barney gasped for air. The back of his neck prickled as he heard his name.

"He's called Jones. Barney Jones. Must go—"

Barney closed his eyes and waited for the man to go. He heard the phone bleep and the sound of it being returned to a pocket with the jangle of coins, then all went silent. He waited, wondering if it was safe to emerge, when suddenly the door was pulled from him and the man's face pushed right up to his. Blazing eyes burned into him as the man hissed a spray of spearmint saliva.

"You didn't think I'd seen you, eh? Wrong. I saw the door move in the mirror. Unlucky. You're not as clever as you thought. I always knew you were trouble. So now it's a change of plan. Get ready for a rough ride, lad – you're coming with me."

CHAPTER 5

Firmly gripping Barney's elbow and with forceful strides, the security officer marched him back to the room where Elaine sat waiting, squinting into her mirror and applying yet more mascara to her panda eyes.

"Sit down, son," he barked. "This unaccompanied minor of yours has a habit of listening to private phone calls and going into restricted areas for staff only. He needs close watching."

Elaine giggled nervously. "Oops. I said he could use the loo. Sorry, Geoff."

"Hold on a minute!" Barney had been trying to obey his rule of keeping quiet but there was no way he could stand back and be accused. He stood up and grabbed his bag. "I'm not staying here to be blamed for anything. If you have weird phone calls when I happen to be around, you can't blame me if I hear all that stuff. Maybe it's time for me to make a phone call myself right now."

He reached into his bag as the officer grabbed his arm.

"No you don't, son. You're calling no one."

"But you were talking to someone about me. I heard you. It sounded well out of order to me."

"You heard nothing of the sort. You've got completely the wrong end of the stick. But it's up to you, lad. If you want to make a fuss about it, we can go through the formal channels. That means you'll miss your plane and have to spend the whole night here, with the high probability of lengthy airport police interviews and the risk of hefty fines for wrongful accusations. A full strip-search might well be necessary. And you won't like that, I can promise you. Or you can keep that mouth of yours shut, forget the whole thing and get on the plane right now. The choice is yours."

Elaine looked at her watch before spraying a mist of perfume behind her ears.

"We really do need to go right now if you want this flight, Barney. If not, just think of the paperwork." She clicked her bag shut and straightened her scarf.

"But I smell a rat," Barney said, looking straight at the security officer, who gave a wry smile and said, "That's no way to talk about Elaine's expensive French perfume."

"Charming, I'm sure." She giggled, giving a playful flick to the man's arm. "Now, shall we go and get you nicely settled in your seat, Barney?"

He shrugged his shoulders. "Just get me on the plane." He sighed, then scowled. "Whatever's going on, I just want to get out of here. If you ask me, it's not just your perfume that smells funny."

"You'd know all about that, kid," the man snarled. "Just make sure you never come my way again. You're trouble and the only thing that stinks around here is your attitude. I won't forget your face so you'd better make sure you don't show it anywhere near me again. You might be able to ponce about on some pansy trampoline but I could flatten you with one blow. I've got trophies for boxing so don't cross me again, got it?"

He turned, pulled at the door violently and strode off through the milling crowd.

"Shall we be off then, poppet?" Elaine smiled, as if nothing at all had happened. She tilted her head to listen to a garbled announcement echoing through the airport.

"It sounds as if they're about to board so we'll just sail right through and get you comfy. Have you got your ticket, sweetheart?"

He handed it to her, confused and still angry, staring sulkily at the door.

"You've got a seat by the window, pet. That's nice, eh?"

He strapped his bag over his shoulder and followed her across the departure lounge and out through the glass doors. Her heels clip-clopped across the tarmac, the plane stretched in front of them and she tottered up the aircraft steps to the open door.

"Hiya, Alan," she sang to the steward checking boarding passes. "This one's a U.M. Seat E10."

"No probs." Alan smiled, running his fingers through his tinted hair and winking. "Enjoy your flight, young man."

"I'll try," Barney said and he made his way down the empty plane towards row 10.

"I'll be around," Elaine told him, while pushing his bag in the overhead locker. "So just give me a nod if you need me. You'll be fine. Nothing to worry about."

He looked out of the window onto the wing. *That's handy*, he thought, *I'm just behind the emergency exit. I can leap out if Alan winks at me again.*

Passengers began moving down the aisle and filling the seats – all but the one next to him. Alan was just about to pull the door shut when a short, stocky woman in a polka-dot headscarf appeared in front of him. She stared around the plane, peering over the top of her red-framed glasses. Barney watched her shuffle down the aisle towards him. The only empty seat was next to his. He smiled. "Row ten by any chance?"

She sighed as she reached up to the locker to put her bag inside before sitting beside him. After fiddling with her seat belt, she took off her glasses, revealing a silver ring through her eyebrow. As she sighed again, Barney gave her a quick look and another smile. "You just made it," he said, as the door slammed shut. "Now you can relax."

"Yes." She didn't look at him.

"You seem a bit nervous. Flying isn't so scary when you get used to it," he said.

"That's a relief." She leaned to look past him through the window.

"You can't see much," Barney said. "Just the wing. They've put arrows on it to show us where to climb out if there's a crisis. Very reassuring, isn't it?"

"Are you alone?" she asked, wiping her face with a tissue.

"I'm a U. M. – that's an 'unaccompanied minor'. It just means they let me on the plane first. Elaine holds my hand if I get upset; she's one of the stewards. What it really means is that they probably think I'll throw a strop. Mum keeps saying I'm at a tricky age but I guess she's thought that since I was two."

The woman gave him a sideways glance but said nothing. As the plane began moving along the tarmac towards the runway, Barney peered out of the window at the runway lights. "Some people get in a flap about flying. I really like it. It must be great to be a pilot."

The engines roared, the plane vibrated as it quickly gained speed and the runway rumbled below. The ground suddenly dropped away beneath them, the airport lights flashed past and Barney felt himself being thrust back into his seat.

"Wow – just feel that power!" he said, giving her another quick smile.

The woman had her eyes shut and her hands gripped the armrests. As the plane climbed steeply and he felt his ears pop, Barney leaned towards her and spoke reassuringly. "You can relax now. That's the scary bit over. We'll be landing in fifty minutes. You'll love that bit."

"I doubt it," she said. For the first time, she turned to look at Barney directly. She had deep-set eyes and fine, pencilled orange eyebrows. Barney noticed the ring through one of them had a tiny snake's head with a pinhead of pink glass for the eye. *Unusual*, he thought.

"Can I ask you a big favour?" she whispered.

"I suppose you want me to shut up, don't you?" he said. "Sorry if I prattle on a bit. I guess I get a bit nervous myself, if I'm honest. That makes me talk a lot. I hope I didn't make you feel worse. It's just that I've had a bit of a tricky time myself just now. The security guy had it in for me. I'm still a bit wound-up about it all, actually."

"It's OK." She smiled. "You've been very friendly and cute. You haven't worried me at all. I think that steward scares me more than anything. He looks about sixteen and utterly terrified. That doesn't give you much confidence, does it? The thing is, I've never been up in one of these things over here before. I'm from the States where airplanes come much bigger and fly far smoother."

"It's a lot gentler when we descend," Barney said. "Er… a favour?"

"Sorry?"

"You asked me for a big favour."

"Ah, yes. You wouldn't happen to have any tissues, would you? I've run out and my eyes keep watering for some reason."

"Same here. I've had a fit of the snuffles since Elaine sprayed her perfume all over the place. I'll have a look in my bag. I might have a few tissues stuffed in the inside pocket."

He squeezed past her and reached up to the locker. As soon as he unzipped his bag, he gasped. His hand touched the cold brass of his trophy stuffed under a t-shirt. "Blimey, it's back in here," he muttered to himself. "That's weird. My address label's come off my bag as well. Mum always insists that goes on after I lost a rucksack once."

Barney sat down again, clutching the bag in his lap. He passed the woman a tissue with one hand while holding his trophy in the other. "Ergh… there's a blob of chewing gum stuffed round where the gymnast unscrews. It's gross – all wet and slimy. That security bloke needs reporting. I'll get my dad to make a complaint."

He raised his hand to attract Elaine's attention but it was Alan who appeared beside them with a trolley of drinks and biscuits.

"How are you doing, you guys?"

"Can I speak to Elaine, please?" Barney asked.

Alan was more concerned with tidying a stack of plastic cups. "Who?"

The woman butted in. "His minder. The stewardess who's looking after him."

"Elaine," Barney added. "The one who brought me on the plane."

"Sorry, sunshine." Alan shrugged. "Haven't a clue who she was. It's just me and Mandy on this flight. Whoever that woman was who came on with you, she got off as soon as you sat down. Never seen her before. Any drinks? Crisps?"

"Hold on a minute." Barney was unable to keep quiet this time. "My mum paid extra because I'm an unaccompanied minor. It's Elaine's job to look after me. She's been worse than useless. Her revolting perfume has left my eyes streaming and I'm just not impressed if she's cleared off. I've got a problem and something needs sorting."

He was becoming very loud and all eyes were on him, as Alan squirmed in the aisle.

"Tell you what," Alan whispered, fussing with the plastic cups again, "I'll sort it all out for you when we land in Glasgow. Don't worry now, how's that?" He smiled nervously and moved on down the aisle, dropping packets of biscuits in a fluster.

"This Elaine, what did she look like?" the woman asked Barney.

"Blue uniform, red scarf. Loads of make-up, big blonde hair, bright nails and reeking of perfume like toilet cleaner. I've not seen her before but now I think about it, there's something kind of familiar about her."

"In that case," the woman said thoughtfully as she pushed the tissue up her sleeve, "it was her I saw as I came up the steps of the plane. She ran down right past me, carrying a clipboard and a little tartan notebook. I didn't take much notice at the time but she was talking into a phone and I heard just a few words."

"What were they? What was she saying?" Barney was ready for another outburst.

The woman raised her eyebrows and the snake eye appeared to wink at him. "You're not going to like this," she said, "so try not to get on your high horse again."

"Try me."

"I remember her words clearly. She said, 'The kid's onboard but I'm not staying with him a minute longer. Not with his attitude.'"

Barney swore, just as the captain announced they were about to descend into a cold and stormy Glasgow.

CHAPTER 6

The blustery night sky had stolen the moon and stars. Barney peered out through the aircraft window at the moving wing flaps skimming through the mist. He could just see the airport lights in the darkness below as the plane banked before dropping under the last wisps of cloud. As he was wondering about what it must be like to land a plane in a storm, there was a whisper in his ear and a hand on his shoulder.

"Would you like me to take you to Arrivals, sunbeam?" It was Alan, smiling and flicking his quiff.

"It's all right, thanks. I'll manage," Barney said.

The plane rocked and juddered.

"Fair play. See you, young man. I'd better strap myself in. Turbulence never agrees with me."

Alan returned to his seat by the door as the woman next to Barney gripped the armrests and screwed up her eyes. The sound of rain spattering the window was drowned by the drone of the descending undercarriage, as the glinting gash of runway rose up towards them.

"It's like we're just skimming the rooftops," Barney observed, wiping the window.

"Let's hope we keep it that way," the woman muttered.

There was a jolt as the wheels skidded on shiny concrete, rumbled through the spray and juddered at the roar of reverse thrust. The plane slowed, swung off the runway and rolled over puddled tarmac to the airport terminal, before coming to a halt.

"You can open your eyes now," Barney said. "Safe and sound. Wet and windy but safe and sound."

As passengers stood and gathered their bags, Alan squeezed down the aisle to announce, "I'd better let you off first or it'll be more than my job's worth."

"I'll keep my eye on him if you like," the woman said, sounding far more relaxed and cheery. "I'll make sure he doesn't go berserk in the airport or throw a teenage wobbly."

"Brilliant, we haven't got long for our turnaround so that's cool. Cheers." Alan retreated, his sense of relief clear to see.

"Sorry I'm such a burden," Barney called after him, before smiling at the woman, "I'll try to behave even though I've already been abandoned once."

With bags zipped and strapped over their shoulders, Barney and the woman descended the steps in a squall of stinging rain. They ran, with heads down, across the tarmac and up the steps into the airport building. They were in a long glass bridge, with planes parked below on both sides, lit by dazzling arc lights. Workers in fluorescent jackets were loading planes or driving about in little yellow trucks, their reflections dancing over the wet concrete.

Two airport police officers stepped out into the corridor, directing them to a queue.

"Security check. Join the queue. Bags and documents at the ready."

"Is there a problem?" the woman asked.

"Just routine. Please stand still and let the sniffer dogs do their job."

A line of eager spaniels and their uniformed handlers stretched in front of them.

"I hope they're not like my gran's dog," Barney whispered. "I don't want a cold nose where it's not needed!"

"You what, lad?" A security officer looked particularly agitated.

"Nothing. Just thinking. Clever, aren't they? Dogs, I mean. I like to see working dogs doing their stuff. My gran's got one."

The man stopped writing on his clipboard and looked up.

"And why would your gran have a sniffer dog?"

Barney laughed at the thought. "No, not a sniffer dog. A guide dog. Golden Labrador. It's cool how they concentrate so hard – like yours there. Come to think of it, Gran would probably like hers to be a sniffer dog too. Then Melda wouldn't just take her round Tesco but also sniff out the best cannabis."

The man stared with eyes like daggers. "You what?"

"Just a joke." Barney smiled. There was an embarrassed silence.

"It's not a laughing matter, young man. This is serious."

"This way, son." Another officer waved him over to a woman in a fluorescent yellow jacket, with a dog on a lead. "Stand still, legs apart and don't distract the dog. Has anyone given you anything to carry? Has your bag been out of your possession at any time?"

Barney said it hadn't, as the officer unzipped his bag and peered inside while a wagging spaniel looked up hopefully. Turning to speak to the American woman from the plane, Barney was surprised to see her further back in the queue, fiddling with her phone.

"Bit of a smell in your bag, laddie," one of the security guards said. "Enough to make the dog's eyes water. It's like deodorant with disinfectant. I wish my son would use that!"

The spaniel seemed to step back in disgust, pause for a moment, then look up.

"What's this trophy, son?"

"For trampolining."

He wasn't impressed. "Move along, now."

One by one, passengers shuffled through the security cordon as passports, tickets and luggage were scrutinised by unsmiling officials and far cheerier spaniels. The dogs looked on, alert and keen, but so far unimpressed by the lack of exciting substances.

Barney had been aware that the woman from the plane at the back of the queue had been recording his interrogation on her phone but by the time he'd been cleared, repacked his bag and moved into the arrivals area, she was nowhere to be seen. He was on his own again and, just as he'd feared, his dad was nowhere among the rows of smiling faces waiting to greet their loved ones.

"Typical," he muttered. "Abandoned again."

He said something stronger when he called him on his phone and got no reply. At least he was cheered by a text from his friend Laura, wishing him the best of luck in getting cash from his dad for the school Disneyland Paris trip.

"Do you want some chips?" Barney looked up to see the American woman looking down at him. "I think we both deserve something after our ordeals, don't you? I need to celebrate getting through the flight. Thanks for looking after me. I'll pay for whatever you want."

"How about a trip to Disneyland Paris?" Barney looked at his watch. "Yeah, why not? Dad will probably be hours yet. Thanks." They walked to the café and sat at a table. As they sipped their drinks and crunched their fries, Barney looked the woman in the eyes and asked, "So why were you recording me on your phone going through security?"

She paused, wiped her mouth with a tissue and leaned forward. "OK, I'll tell you straight. I'm the casting director for a studio in Hollywood. I'm looking for a guy about your age and height for a big movie. If my director likes the look of you, you could get the part. Big money. What do you think of that?"

Barney frowned. "What makes you think I can act? Don't get me wrong, the money would be great for Disneyland Paris but shouldn't you ask first before you go round filming random kids? Actually, it's weird because a couple of weeks ago, a woman who was pretending to be blind asked me if I…" He stopped and thoughtfully bit a chip very slowly.

"She asked if you what?"

Barney sat back looking completely puzzled. "That's so weird. I've only just realised. There was something about her – just like Elaine. Blimey, I think she *was* Elaine."

"Elaine?"

"That stewardess who disappeared. I think I'd better report this to the desk over there. Something really weird is going on."

"I'm sure there must be a perfectly logical explanation," she said impatiently.

He stood up, picked up his bag and drained his glass. "Thanks for the chips. I need to go and tell the airline about their staff – that security guy and that Elaine. Something's not right and I reckon it's up to me to make a bit of a fuss."

"Say honey, why don't you just think about my movie offer? I'll give you a call. Can I have your number and address? Just say when you're heading back through here and I could meet you again. When you're signed up by the studio you'll get an advance of several thousand dollars even before shooting begins."

"To be honest," he called over his shoulder as he headed back to the concourse, "I've got something else on my mind right now. It's called 'stranger danger'."

The woman snatched a phone from her leopard-print bag as Barney headed towards the enquiries desk. She darted to a corner and hissed anxiously, her voice urgent, agitated and with no hint of an American accent. "Bring the car to the entrance. He's not taking the bait. We'll have to use force. Be quick – but remember, he's smart."

She threw the phone in her bag and marched through the crowds towards the enquiries desk, where

Barney had just caught the attention of a man at a computer.

"Excuse me, but I've just landed here and I'm an unaccompanied minor and—"

"Hold on a sec, laddie. I've just got to enter this data and I'll be right with you."

The man didn't look up from the screen but Barney didn't give up. "The thing is, the more I think about it, the more I think something scary is going on—"

The man paused to look up. "Scary? How do you mean?"

Before Barney could say any more, the woman swept him away. "Come on, love. Sorry about this but we're in a hurry." She dragged him towards the doors. "I'll explain everything just out here. Please just come with me now – there's something I must tell you."

Hurriedly shuffling Barney through the automatic doors, she waved at an approaching car that squealed to a halt at the kerb. Barney pulled away but she grabbed his bag.

"Just listen to me a minute. I'll explain." She tried to pull him towards the car but he resisted.

"I don't know who you are but just leave me alone." He was shouting and people stared. Suddenly the woman's tactics changed so dramatically that Barney was completely taken by surprise and stared at her, stunned.

"You assaulted me, you horrible child. You tried to rob my purse and I'm making a citizen's arrest. Get in that car." Its back door was already open and its engine was revving.

A man walking past stopped to offer her help. "Are you OK, love? Kids like him should be locked up."

"He's been trouble the whole flight." She was almost screaming, "This kid shouldn't be allowed to fly on his own. He's nothing but trouble and he should be arrested."

"Barney – whatever's going on?" Barney looked up to see his dad emerging through the gathering crowd. "What have you done?"

The woman swore and suddenly ran to the car, threw herself onto the back seat and slammed the door as the vehicle roared off into the traffic.

"It's disgraceful," someone shouted. "Kids like that shouldn't be allowed out on their own to upset decent passengers. Teenagers today are out of control."

As the crowd dispersed, several people muttered about the state of young people and useless parents letting kids travel alone. Barney and his dad were left facing each other in the rain, frowning in awkward silence.

"Dad – it's not like it looks."

"Whatever's going on, Barney?"

"To be honest, Dad, I'm not really sure."

"Great, just great. Absolutely terrific. Just what the hell have you done this time?"

CHAPTER 7

Barney's dad opened the car door with a frustrated sigh. "I just don't know what's got into you lately. We didn't bring you up to argue and be so awkward."

As soon as Barney sat in the passenger's seat, his temper finally flared. "Listen to me, Dad. That woman was well weird and a total nutcase. They all were. There were three of them and they all had it in for me… Why won't you believe me that I've done nothing wrong?"

His dad sighed again. "After parents' evening I thought you were going to make a real effort to improve things. We agreed."

Barney tried to explain everything – the security officer, Elaine and the American woman with all her Hollywood talk – before he heard himself say, "Actually, she was trying to kidnap me."

His dad swung round to face him. "Don't talk such rubbish, Barney. You read too much of that kidnap stuff. You know very well your teacher said your imagination is much too vivid. And what if that woman really was from Hollywood? She could have been genuine and changed your life! Why must you always be suspicious of people? I blame your mother, putting ideas into your head that everyone's out to get you. That and all your fantasy books about crime and boy wizards. I suppose the next thing you'll tell me is that the pilot was a zombie married to a vampire with a brother who's a werewolf. Just get real, Barney."

"But Dad, I'm not making it up, honest. You saw that car roar off. She was trying to get me inside and—"

"That's enough, Barney. Don't you dare say any more. Get it out of your head immediately. Don't mention it ever again – especially to your mother. You know how paranoid she is about you flying up here. If you tell her about this she'll stop you coming up here all together. Is that what you want, eh?"

Like the windscreen wipers slapping rhythmically in front of their eyes, his words drummed through Barney's head, building to a crescendo until the car screeched to a halt at traffic lights. His dad swore, knocked the gear lever into neutral, wrenched the handbrake and sighed yet again. "We agreed last time I saw you that your behaviour has got to change, Barney. Let's make it start right now. We can't go on like this."

Barney had said nothing for the last few miles, still feeling numb and confused. But he couldn't let his dad go unchallenged.

"Maybe if you'd been on time, I'd have been all right. Then again, I should be used to you never being there for me – yet still I have to take all the blame. As always."

Barney knew he'd scored a direct hit with that one. His dad went very quiet and for the rest of the journey neither of them spoke a word. The wipers did all the talking. Barney stared at the driving rain in the headlights, the depressingly gloomy streets and traffic lights blinking from swirling puddles. He knew only too well that nothing short of a miracle would be able to salvage this disastrous weekend.

Eventually, as they pulled into the drive, his dad said calmly, "I'm sorry I was late, Barney. You're right, I should have been there to meet you. I got held up in the traffic when I fetched Gran."

"Gran?" Barney's eyes lit up. "Is she here at your house?"

"Didn't I tell you she wanted to see you? Well, not so much see you as get up to your usual mischief together. I couldn't keep her away when I told her you were coming."

"Brilliant!"

His look said it all. *Maybe the weekend won't be quite so bad after all.*

Gran was as lively as ever. She threw her arms around Barney and giggled in his ear. "It's great to see you again, love. Not that I can, but I can smell you good enough!" Melda went wild with excitement, thrashing him with her tail and licking his face.

"At least someone appreciates me," he said.

"I'll just put the kettle on," his dad said half-heartedly, lumbering into the kitchen.

"Do I sense a bit of an atmosphere, dear?"

"We've had a few words, Gran. I'm in disgrace, I'm afraid. I'm at that funny age."

"I've been at a funny age for years, dear! Your father's always telling me off. Now come on, tell me how you're getting on with all that trampolining. I bet you're doing wonders."

"Actually, I'm really chuffed. I've just won a trophy. In fact, I've got it here – to show Dad that I'm not a complete waster."

"I'm sure he's proud of you, love. We all are. I'd love to see it – well, touch it, at any rate."

Barney took the trophy from his bag. "I'll just have to scrape something off it first."

He used a tissue to remove the gum and handed the trophy to her proudly.

"I wish your father had done some sport or competitions at your age. He was hard work as a boy. Come to think of it, he always had a bit of an attitude problem. Still has!"

"Really?" Barney was already feeling much better, as he watched Gran's fingers feel every detail of the little gymnast figure on his trophy.

"This is excellent. I love the feel of this. Quite heavy. Unusual smell. What's the base made of? It seems fairly solid."

"It's only hollow. Not solid gold, I'm afraid."

"Don't be silly, dear. I might be getting on a bit, but I can tell if something's solid or not. I tell you, this base isn't hollow at all."

"Well, it was when that guy at the airport took it off me…" He told her the whole story, including the strange phone conversation he'd overheard in the toilets and all the rest.

"Well, that's it, then," Gran said, picking up the trophy again. "Someone's put something inside the base. Go on, Barney – untwist it and take a look."

Barney began to rotate the little brass gymnast. It unscrewed easily and he lifted it off the base, revealing a small hole. "I can't really see inside." He put a newspaper on the floor and upturned the base, pouring out a pile of white granules.

"It's full of sugar... or something..." Barney bent down to smell it just as his dad walked in with a tin of biscuits.

"Barney! Whatever do you think you're doing? Don't tell me you're into this stuff now. Where did you get it, for God's sake?"

"Dad, I know you've got a low opinion of me but I'm not a crack dealer, honest. This stuff was inside my trophy. Do you think it could be drugs? I reckon it was planted on me. I tell you, it was that horrible security guy before I got on the plane."

"In which case, this needs reporting. You could've got in serious trouble. I'm going to phone the police. But please, Barney, you must say if there's anything you've been hiding from me."

"No, Dad. I'm happy to tell the police everything. Nothing to hide. I'm an angel, really."

"You've just had a bit of a scene at the airport, Barney. You're hardly a model angel, are you?"

Gran, as always, rushed to Barney's defence. "An angel with an ASBO! But still an angel at heart, eh? Just a little misunderstanding, that's all."

The police were extremely interested in every aspect of Barney's experience at the airport and questioned him with great suspicion. He had to write a statement and, much to his annoyance, they took away his trophy with the mystery substance. Just as an officer was filling in a form in the front room, Gran insisted on Barney retrieving the blob of chewing gum from the bin.

"There'll be saliva in that chewing gum. DNA. I listen to lots of crime audiobooks, you see. I've just finished *Kiss of Death*, where they caught the killer from lip prints on the victim's leather glove."

"You'll find real life crime isn't quite like the books and TV, madam. I'll take it away for analysis but I doubt it will lead to much." Stretching a latex glove over his fingers like a surgeon about to perform a delicate operation, the police officer picked up the tissued blob and placed it inside a small plastic bag, which he carefully sealed and labelled.

"Just consider yourself fortunate that a sniffer dog didn't pick up on your little lot. You'd have been held for questioning all night."

"So how come the dogs didn't smell the drugs in Barney's trophy?" Gran asked.

"Good question. They're normally very sharp. They'll often pick up the tiniest speck even if it's in another room, even if sealed in a container. Mind you, we don't know yet what this stuff is. It could be harmless. Let's hope so, eh?"

Barney's dad had remained very quiet throughout all the questioning before he asked, "What about the person who planted it on Barney? Do you think you can get him?"

"Hard to say. We'll certainly try to get to the bottom of all this. If a criminal offence has been committed then

Barney here could well be required to testify in a court of law. He may be required for further questioning or indeed to identify any suspects. It all remains to be seen."

Barney had another thought. "What happens if I see that guy when I go back home on Sunday? He could still be there."

"Just report it at the airport. Don't even speak to the man."

"I hope you don't think my grandson is a bad lad, officer," Gran said.

"Don't worry, madam. He seems perfectly reasonable to me. Believe me, I've seen far worse."

Even Barney's dad managed to smile at that.

Much later, after a particularly large takeaway, they sat on the sofa with Melda sprawled and snoring at their feet. With Barney's dad engrossed in the news, Gran whispered in Barney's ear.

"Do you want to see my latest gadget?"

"Oh no, what have you got this time, Gran?"

"Have you got your phone? Give me a call and watch what happens."

Barney tapped in her number and winced at the terrible noise. Melda leapt up with a yelp, wagged her tail and held Gran's elbow in her mouth.

Barney's dad looked up, amazed. "How did the dog know to do that?"

"I trained her. You see, I didn't hear it either. I bet Barney did. Only dogs and youngsters can hear it. The ring tone is called Teenbuzz. It's what's known as a mosquito alarm that no one over thirty can hear. They play it outside places to get rid of teenagers hanging around. But the lad next door put it on my phone for me so now I can leave it switched on wherever I am and even if it goes off in a funeral, no one minds a bit! Melda knows just to give me a gentle nudge on the elbow. Then I know I've got a phone message. Clever, isn't it?"

"It might not disturb anyone when it rings," Barney's dad began, "but I bet everyone knows about it when you start chatting at the top of your voice, Mum!"

"Not necessarily, dear. It could be someone just leaving a voicemail or whatever they call it. Very handy. What do you think, Barney?"

"It's cool. Can I copy it for my phone? Then you can call me in the middle of Mrs Peters's lessons and she'll never know!"

"I don't think that's a good idea, Barney." His dad frowned.

"And what about this to stop me getting lost?" Gran went on, slipping onto each hand two blue plastic rings. "I just get someone to tap into this little sat nav the postcode of wherever I want to go, and the rings tell me how to get there. If I need to turn right, the right hand ring vibrates. To go left, the left hand ring vibrates. If I miss a turn, both rings vibrate so I stop and it tells me where to go. It's very useful for finding places around town."

"That's really clever," Barney said. "I could do with that for when I ride my bike – when I get a paper round."

"Then I'll see what I can do for you, dear."

"When are you thinking of getting a paper round?" His dad didn't sound too happy about it.

"When I can. I need some money for when I go on school trips. Like Disneyland Paris."

"Who said you're going? I told you that I need to think about it. You've got to make a few changes, remember? You can't expect Mrs Peters to take you anywhere without a few promises, Barney."

Gran whispered, "Don't worry, love – we'll work on him."

"I heard that, mother."

"Good. You were meant to. I've already decided to treat you to Sunday lunch. And when you're full-up and contented, Barney will ask you if he can go to Disneyland Paris with his school. But in the meantime I fancy a game of cards. How about it, Barney? I've got some smart new Braille playing cards."

"If you like, Gran, but I'll beat you. No sweat!"

"No you won't. You're going to wear a blindfold and learn to read Braille. Then we're on equal terms. I hope you remember some of the letters and numbers I taught you last time."

"Yeah, I reckon so. Let's give it a go."

Barney in his blindfold and Gran with a second glass of white wine were soon giggling and playing raucously. Although Barney was far slower than Gran at reading the tiny raised patterns on the cards, he managed to beat her after a few rounds. It was very late before the game was finally declared a tie and all retired to bed in high spirits. Even Barney's dad was unusually jolly and

Barney's last hope, as his head touched the pillow, was for a better day tomorrow. He'd try extra hard and make a superhuman effort to impress. His attitude would sparkle like never before. All being well, he wouldn't have to give another thought to those undesirable characters from his bewildering journey. But hopes, as he knew only too well, could so easily be dashed.

CHAPTER 8

The sun sparkled on a shimmering Loch Lomond and on the purple heather covering the mountains beyond. Looking out through huge plate glass windows from the restaurant, Barney watched boats and windsurfers being buffeted by the biting breeze just beyond the jetty.

"Lemon cheesecake, anyone?" Barney's dad glanced at the menu, still in a cheerful mood after Saturday's trip to town, a winning round of golf and their evening at the cinema.

"Cheers, Dad. I can't believe I'm looking out at this great view, while tomorrow I'll be back in Mrs Peters's boring classroom. This weekend has really flown by."

"It's been great fun, Barney," his Gran said. "Even if I didn't quite beat you at cards."

"When you come back in a couple of weeks, I'll take you to the rugby, Barney," his dad said enthusiastically but then added, less cheerily, "but careful how you go on the plane, eh? No more drug smuggling! I'll let you know when the police return your trophy and tell me any news. And make sure you try hard with your school work."

He handed Barney an envelope. "That's the deposit for the Disneyland Paris trip."

"Wow – thanks, Dad!"

"But remember the rest only follows if you behave and keep that attitude in order."

"Yeah, 'course." Barney put the envelope in his pocket and took out his phone. "I promised Laura I'd let her know if I managed to melt your heart." He texted:

```
C U in Paris
```

and then sat back grinning. "Now, how about that cheesecake?

The airport seemed quieter than on Friday evening. Fewer passengers were waiting in the cafés and shops. Barney's dad delivered him to the desk, they said their goodbyes and a steward took him to the waiting plane.

"I'm Debbie." The steward beamed. "And I'll be looking after you from now on."

"Do you know Elaine?" Barney asked. "She should have been my steward on the journey here."

"I can't say I do," Debbie answered, looking puzzled. "Which is strange as I thought I knew all the girls on these flights. There again, staff are always coming and going. Now, if you'd like to get settled in your seat, I'll pop your bag in the locker and we'll soon be off."

Other passengers began to board, including a tall boy with a purple designer rucksack. He made a beeline down the plane, opened the locker above Barney's head, pushed in his rucksack and, after fumbling inside for a while, he promptly sat beside Barney, with a jolly, "Hi, I'm Seb."

Somewhat startled, Barney looked up from the airline magazine he'd been skimming. "Er... hi."

"On your own?" The boy had a mop of black hair and wore tartan knee-length shorts. He didn't wait for a reply. "Me too. I'm used to it. I do this most weekends. I've done it for years. I meet all sorts. I like Debbie. She's one of the best."

"Not like Elaine," Barney heard himself say.

"I've never come across that one. New, is she?"

"I don't know. She was on duty on Friday. Except she disappeared. The other steward was a guy called Alan."

"You want to watch him. He gives me the creeps. I have to say, I wouldn't like their job. They don't get paid much, you know. And you get some really weird passengers."

"Thanks."

"No, not you. Dodgy types. I've seen all sorts. Did you know there was a terrorist attack here a while back? A jeep smashed into the main doors and burst into flames. Luckily the firebomb didn't go off. But from then on the security guys have been real twitchy."

"Yeah, I've noticed!"

The plane began moving towards the runway, as Seb whispered above the safety talk. "I hope you don't mind me asking, but have you ever been searched by security?"

"Sure. It's a long story…" As soon as they were airborne, Barney recounted every detail. He finished with, "So I've no idea what that stuff was inside my trophy. I've yet to find out. I'll just be extra careful next time."

"Next time?" Seb's eyes widened. "You mean you fly this way often?

"Now and again."

Seb leaned very close to him. "Can I just ask you something?" His whisper was so quiet that Barney could hardly hear. "If I asked you to bring something with you next time, would you do it? It's only a little something – just like a teabag sewn under the collar. It's totally undetectable but you'd get paid a grand. Dead easy for a thousand quid. Think about it. It's a doddle."

Barney stared at him, open-mouthed. "Is that what you do? Are you some sort of smuggler?"

"Maybe." He winked.

"What is it? What do you carry?"

"That would be telling. Well, would you?"

"No way. Apart from the risk, it's wrong. You don't know who you'd be harming."

"Does that mean..." Seb paused thoughtfully, "you're going to shop me?"

"What if I did? What have I got to lose?"

Seb smiled. "I like you!" He shook Barney's hand. "You're a cool kid."

Barney watched him carefully and said, "Sniffer dogs will soon find that stuff. Then you'll be kept all night being questioned. Is that what you really want? Things could get nasty."

Seb looked away. He picked up a magazine and thumbed through, saying nothing for a while. The pilot announced they were about to descend and to fasten all seat belts.

"So will you?" Seb asked furtively.

"Will I what?"

"Will you consider it?"

"What, reporting you? It would probably be for your own good. Or would you send round the heavy mob and have me beaten up? You can certainly forget about trying to rope me in to your little game. It stinks. To be honest, I'm getting fed-up with being made weird offers by strangers at airports."

"Fair play, Barney. You're sound. At least I know where I stand. Fancy a fruit gum?"

He pointed a tube of sweets at Barney, who stared back, uncertain what to make of the boy. *Rather overconfident*, he thought.

"No thanks. I don't like green ones – just red. How old are you, Seb?"

"Seventeen."

"Then you should know better."

The plane juddered on the runway. Seb looked Barney in the eyes – and for the first time his confidence seemed to waver.

"Better than what?"

"You just called me Barney. How do you know my name? I never told you my name, not once. Debbie didn't say it either. How did you know?" There was a long and awkward pause.

"I'll tell you later." Seb stood to collect his rucksack as the plane came to a halt at the terminal. He didn't stop talking as they walked into the airport and through an arcade of shops, many of which were just closing. Debbie led the way, past a clattering shutter being pulled across a newsagents.

"In an hour or so, this place will be like a morgue,"

Seb continued. "I had to spend all night here once. Snow grounded all the flights. It was heaving with bodies sleeping all over the floor."

Debbie walked ahead as Seb grabbed Barney's elbow and whispered, "Just act normally."

"What's up?"

"Ahead. Two security guys. Walking this way. Don't say a word, right?"

Barney stopped walking. "Seb, I don't know who you are or what you're doing. If you've got something to hide, that's your problem. Don't drag me into anything, thank you."

The security officers were a few steps away when one of them looked straight at them.

"I'd like a word, lads."

"It's OK, they're with me." Debbie smiled.

"Maybe, love. But one of them could be of interest to us."

Barney looked at Seb for a reaction but was stunned to hear what came next.

"We're looking for a Barney Jones on the flight from Glasgow."

"This is him," Seb said, flashing an ID card under their noses.

"Is there a problem?" Debbie asked. "I'm meant to deliver him to his mother at the desk."

"Leave him with us, love. Don't worry – he couldn't be in more secure hands."

It was only Seb who laughed nervously. Debbie hesitated before shrugging and turning to walk away.

"OK, then. Nice to have met you, boys. See you again. Bye."

"Just step this way, son," one of the security officers said, gesturing towards a door marked 'PRIVATE'. "You can go now, Seb. It's just the lad she wants."

Seb raised his hand. "Cheers! See you again, Barney. All the best. Good luck."

He headed off towards the stairs, leaving Barney totally bewildered.

"What's going on?" he asked, but it was perfectly clear that neither officer had any intention of offering the slightest hint of an explanation. Barney stood facing a door, with no idea of what was on the other side. The officer tapped four numbers on the digital lock and the door clicked open.

"In you go, young man."

Barney entered a small, brightly lit room with no windows. There was a table in the middle, with orange plastic chairs around it, a computer on a desk by a filing cabinet, and a plasma screen mounted on the wall above it. Another security officer in a fluorescent jacket sat at the desk, wearing headphones, but all Barney could see was the back of his head and a gun at his waist. A woman, somewhere in her forties, sat at the table working on a laptop, with a pile of box files beside her. She looked up as Barney entered and, without smiling, said brusquely, "Sit down."

Barney did as he was told, without taking his eyes off the woman, who was particularly tiny, he thought. She was smartly dressed in a navy blue suit, with short black hair and piercing blue eyes, with a smear of lilac eye shadow. Her voice had an abrupt northern edge to it, sounding serious and authoritative. Whoever she was, he could tell she meant business.

"Firstly, I'd like to see your passport."

He handed it to her, she glanced at it and then looked up. "Right, Barnaby Jones. There are a number of issues we need to discuss. I need to point out that this interview is being recorded." She pointed at a camera fixed on the wall behind her before nodding at the two security officers, who promptly turned and left, shutting the door behind them.

"Your mother knows you will be late so we'll be here as long as it takes. I also need to make it clear that I want some straight answers to some straight questions. Do you understand? In short, I want the truth."

Barney was confused and scared. This woman made Mrs Peters seem like a cuddly lamb.

"What have I done?" he croaked.

"That's for me to determine," she said. "I work for the government. Internal Security. A very serious incident has occurred, to which you were a party. But I need to make something very clear from the outset. Under no circumstances are you to tell anyone, I repeat, *anyone*, of the information you are about to hear. I need your signature on this piece of paper, which is the Official Secrets Act. Basically, it means you are bound by law to keep your mouth shut about everything we discuss, do you understand? I will not hesitate to have you instantly arrested if you divulge anything to anyone at anytime."

She passed him the paper and a pen and waited for him to sign on the dotted line. He glanced at the sea of print on the page. It meant nothing but he signed it anyway.

"The Glasgow Police," she went on, "contacted my department with the utmost urgency regarding the substance you carried on an aircraft and right through Glasgow airport."

"I didn't know about it," Barney said. "I didn't have a clue. I've never seen drugs before."

She stared at him, long and hard. "We're not talking about drugs. The substance hidden in your hand-luggage was TATP. Do you know what that is?"

Barney shook his head.

"It's a chemical called triacetone triperoxide." She waited for a reaction but seeing his blank expression, she continued. "It is highly dangerous and you had enough to blow up the plane."

Barney stared at her, horrified.

"And what is more," she added, staring right into his eyes, "it is very volatile. In other words, it is unstable and easily explodes. Had you emptied it in your father's house beside the gas fire or a naked flame, there'd be no house left. Nor you, for that matter."

Barney could only croak, "Crikey!"

"This explosive has been used by terrorists to make bombs in the past and—"

"But I'm not a terrorist!" Barney interrupted. "I'm just a normal kid."

"I am fully aware of that. My officers have done their research all weekend. We now know everything about you: date of birth the tenth of April, born in Cardiff, only child, one grandparent, appendix removed aged six, parents divorced when aged seven, living with mother, Gwyneth, a district nurse who drives a silver Mazda, registration number… I needn't go on but we even know about the two helpings of lemon cheesecake at Loch Lomond at lunchtime today." Her face remained stern, with what seemed to be a permanent frown. Barney couldn't believe what he was hearing.

"However do you know that?"

"It's my business to know. Like your taste in fruit gums. Red but not green."

Barney stared at her but she read his mind, pointing to the man at the desk behind her. "That's right, we were listening in. It's all recorded. Your whole conversation on the plane."

"So you know about Seb? Why didn't you have him arrested?"

"He works for us. You dealt with him well. I asked him to wind you up a bit. You impressed me, especially when he made a mistake and called you by name. So it's all right, I know you're not a threat and just an innocent victim. You displayed a healthy sense of right and wrong so I need your help. You were unwittingly used by – let's call them 'an unknown group' – and you could be crucial to tracking them down. It's vital we find out more about them and that's where you come in."

"What do you want me to do?" For the first time Barney felt the pressure lift slightly, despite the woman's steely stare and no-nonsense manner.

"We have a number of suspects I want you to confirm for us. Look carefully at the screen where you'll see images from CCTV cameras of the day you flew to Glasgow. You'll see yourself, other passengers and various staff. I want you to pick out those you spoke to."

The large screen on the wall fizzed into life, showing queues of waiting passengers, customers in airport shops and others being searched by security staff.

"That's me, there," Barney said. "I'm removing my belt. And that's him – the security man called Geoff. He's the one who took away my trophy then returned it to my bag."

The screen zoomed in to show the man's sweaty face close-up. "You can just see the shape of Australia on his head."

The woman looked up at the screen. "We realise he wasn't genuine. After you boarded the plane, he disappeared without trace. It was his first day at the airport and we now know he got the job by using stolen ID. We're sure he was on the look-out for an unsuspecting passenger to target – like an unaccompanied minor. You were clearly ideal. He only needed a few minutes to get the explosive into your trophy, then he somehow returned it to your bag without you knowing."

"It was when I went to wash my hands," Barney said.

The woman continued. "We think it was all a plot to test the security system before they strike for real. It seems they planted TATP on you to see if the dogs detected it. They used a strong scent inside your bag which worked like a shield and stopped the dogs finding it. Not only that, they sealed it inside your trophy. It wasn't chewing gum stuck on it but an unusual resin containing a plastic explosive known as PETN – or pentaerythritol tetranitrate – which can be easily ignited to devastating effect with a normal cigarette lighter. However, sniffer dogs and vapour detectors usually pick it up – but not in this case. You've certainly alerted us to a new and dangerous threat, so for that reason we're glad we discovered you."

"So how come," Barney asked, "airport security picked our flight to search? It's never happened before."

The woman clicked her pen repeatedly, seeming agitated and impatient. "Glasgow got an anonymous warning that someone on your flight was 'carrying something' so the security police got into action. The gang themselves doubtless sent the message as it was a dry run. They must have sat back, observed and took notes, which means they've now succeeded in finding a way to conceal bomb equipment that is undetectable to sniffer dogs. I need not tell you what kind of serious threat that now poses."

She clicked the pen one last time and threw it on the desk in obvious frustration.

"Do you think Elaine was anything to do with all this?" Barney asked naively.

The woman folded her arms and sighed. "Who?"

"The steward who was meant to look after me on the plane but she disappeared."

"Ah, her. Get her up on the monitor, Mike." Elaine's blurry image filled the screen.

"This one is still something of an enigma," the woman said, "and this is where you can provide more detail. She may look like a dumb blonde but she clearly knew where the security cameras were and kept her face turned away. This is the best we've got of her. Sadly it's too indistinct for face-recognition software."

"I'm sure I'd recognise her again even without her perfume, make-up and big hair."

The woman looked up thoughtfully and, with elbows on the table, clasped her hands and rested her chin on them. "Are you sure? She's doubtless a mistress of disguise."

"I can still see her eyes and teeth in my mind. She couldn't change those, could she?"

"You'd be surprised," she said, her face still cold and emotionless.

"I'm sure it was her who I met before, in a black frizzy wig and dark glasses, pretending to be blind. I think she's got some kind of mark on the back of her hand that she hides with gloves or a plaster. Anyway, I'd certainly know the other woman," Barney added confidently. "I'd never forget her."

The woman's eyes sharpened and her frown deepened. "Who do you mean?"

"The American woman who sat next to me on the plane. I reckon she was involved too. I think she must have been there to watch what happened – to make sure I got searched. After all, she recorded me on her phone with the sniffer dogs. She made me an offer to be in a film and I'm sure she was trying to kidnap me when my dad arrived."

After a pause and a doubtful glance at the man behind her, she said coldly, "We'll run the video and see if you can see her. Run a ticket check, Mike. Get her details."

Barney watched the screen closely, scanning the faces in the queues filing past the airport checkpoints. He recognised a few of the other passengers from his flight.

"Hold on," he shouted. "Rewind a bit. I think that was her."

The screen crackled, the picture reversed frame by frame, until Barney pointed. "There!"

"That's very interesting," the woman said, squinting up at the screen. "This is additional information. You've been helpful to us already. Enhance her face, Mike."

The image sharpened and became perfectly clear. Barney had no doubt who it was. "That's definitely her. You can even see the ring in her eyebrow – like a snake."

"Excellent. That's clear enough for image enhancement and biometric analysis. As good as any fingerprint."

"But she seemed really friendly to begin with. Very normal, in fact."

"Normal enough to fly on a plane in the full knowledge that she was sitting beside a potential firebomb?"

The security officer spoke for the first time, pointing at the computer screen.

"She booked in as Maria Borrelli but her passport number doesn't match with records."

"What does that prove?" Barney asked.

"She was a fraud. False passport. This lot are smart. They know just what they're doing. They left no trace evidence behind anywhere. Your trophy was wiped clean of prints. Just yours and your grandmother's – and a few dog hairs."

Barney jumped up, almost shrieking and startling the woman sitting in front of him.

"Gran! Of course! *Kiss of Death!*"

The security officer turned around, peered over his glasses at Barney and shook his head in bafflement. But neither his disapproving expression nor the steely glare from the woman could dampen Barney's excitement. "The fridge. The fridge."

"You're failing to make the remotest piece of sense," she snapped.

"Down the corridor," Barney gabbled, "in the staff room where I met Elaine, there's a fridge. She threw away her plastic cup but it bounced behind the fridge. It could still be there. I saw her lipstick print on it. There'd be fingerprints, too. Even saliva. DNA."

The security officer snatched a phone and muttered into it as the woman's face brightened for the first time. "If you're right, that could be important trace evidence, to say nothing of valuable profiling information. Now just sit down, Barnaby…"

She paused, sat back in her chair and took a deep breath. "I'll be perfectly straight with you, young man. I was expecting you to be hard work – a bit of a brat, in fact. But you're not. That doesn't mean I like you but I think we could use you. I can tell you're bright and have something about you. You don't exactly live up to your reputation, thankfully. "

"My reputation? How do you mean?"

"I've done my homework. Which, it seems, is more than you do. I've read your school file. Quite a few 'attitudes' in your last report."

"However did you see all that? Don't tell me you know Mrs Peters!"

"No, but I've seen what's on her computer. I asked one of my staff to investigate you yesterday. He's a dab hand at hacking into all sorts. So you see, I was prepared for the worst. Mind you, people with a certain attitude problem like yours seem to be well-suited to the investigation service. Irritating, awkward and rubbing people up the wrong way. You might just have got what it takes."

Barney sat very still but his mind was buzzing. "So… are you spies or something? Like MI5?"

She closed her eyes and sighed. "Spies are for Hollywood films. Never mind who I am. Enough to say I'm part of the SIS. That's the Secret Intelligence Service. We're concerned with threats to national security – hence my involvement in this case. To be honest—" She stopped as the door opened and a security officer entered holding a sealed transparent bag. Inside it Barney could see a plastic cup with a smear of lipstick on the rim. For the first time, the woman in front of him gave just the hint of a smile.

"I'm impressed," she said coolly. "That doesn't happen often – ask my staff."

"I wish you'd tell my dad. I can never seem to impress him."

"No," she snapped severely. "Under no circumstances are you to mention any of this to your parents – or anyone. Do you understand? You've signed the Official Secrets Act."

"I'm not good at keeping my mouth shut, but I'm getting better at it," he said.

"We can train you jn that."

"Sorry?"

"As a result of the last few minutes, I've decided you can be of further use to us. Nothing major, but just a matter of keeping your eyes open and reporting anything suspicious. You've got the right sort of mind. On top of that, there's a cheeky charm about you. It does nothing for me, but I can see that it might work to our benefit in certain places. A young lad with boyish sparkle can sometimes disarm even the hardest of fanatics. You could be useful as a JR, like Seb. That's our jargon for a Juvenile Recruit. We'll contact you in due course. And before you ask – yes, you will be paid. Very well, as it happens. This current unknown gang could well be part of a new international terrorist organisation."

"You mean you want me to work for you as a spy?"

"Don't be absurd. I can't stand that term. It's vulgar. You'll simply be another pair of eyes and ears to report what you see and hear. It might mean spending every so often at an airport to observe what's going on and to engage in a few extra conversations."

"I've had plenty of practice at hanging around airports."

"But not with a listening device, and being paid for the pleasure. In fact, I might team you up with Seb, seeing as you're fairly compatible. We'll inform you when training begins. We already have your mobile phone details. A technician has been analysing your phone after Seb took it from your bag on the plane. You'll get it back in a minute. So all that's left is for you to sign this."

She pushed another piece of paper towards him.

"What is it?"

"Nothing much. Just a legality. It covers us, that's all. In the event of you getting killed."

CHAPTER 9

For all intents and purposes, the tall upright man in a smart black coat was just another tourist. No one would have remembered him from the scandal of a few years before. He stood pompously, with broad shoulders pulled back, his shining bald head held high and with a bearing that couldn't deny his military past. As he stared up at the statue through wolfish eyes he slowly raised his arm to look at an expensive wrist watch through his almost-as-expensive gold-rimmed spectacles.

"You're late," he whispered at an approaching woman, though his dangerous eyes remained fixed on the statue's face. "By forty-eight seconds precisely."

"Geoff's trying to find somewhere to park," she said casually.

He looked down at her briefly before reaching out to caress the statue's feet.

"Must you wear that hideous thing in a place like this?"

"Sorry?"

"Your tacky facial furniture. Inappropriate. If God had intended us to wear rings through our orange eyebrows he would have provided us with perforated temples."

He repositioned a wreath of poppies against the foot of the plinth where a single word 'JENNER' was engraved.

"Was it really necessary to meet here?" the woman remarked abruptly, unimpressed by the surrounding splendour. "They filmed bits of *Harry Potter* here. But never mind Hogwarts; where's the café? I'm starving."

The man sighed and muttered, "Pearls before swine... Such magnificence is clearly wasted on a rough diamond like you, Jan." He pointed up at the marble figure regaled in Georgian academic dress. "Take a long hard look at my hero. A year from now you will have him and me to thank for making you very rich. Doctor Jenner here has driven me for the last five years. He will make us both multi-millionaires."

"But it isn't just the money that's driving you, is it, Brigadier?"

He looked her directly in the eyes. "My ambition is wealth, my engine is revenge. Revenge for a tarnished military reputation."

She smiled. "You were sacked. I read all about your brutal torture of prisoners in Iraq."

His eyes narrowed. "I was effective. And I shall be effective in my revenge."

"Your time in prison seems to have made you even more vicious." She laughed.

"Exactly, my dear." He peered at her over the top of his glasses. "I'm glad to say it was there where I met an equally vicious prison officer. At least I was able to tempt you to leave that job and join my project.

Your cruel streak and respect for no one are just what I need. I know you won't let me down – despite your poor taste in eyebrow jewellery."

He paused as a party of school children with clipboards gathered around the statue for a talk on Edward Jenner – the local country doctor who developed vaccination for smallpox in 1796. The brigadier looked on at the chattering children disapprovingly before moving away.

The woman glanced around before whispering, "So how's the production going? Have the labs delivered the goods?"

"Leave the business side of things to me," he snapped. "You concentrate on strategic planning and operations. I gather the trial run went to plan. You got the TATP through undetected?"

"No problem."

"Good. Now I know we can use undetectable explosives when the time is right. I also gather you used an unaccompanied minor. Whose idea was it to risk using a child?"

The woman turned away, unable to disguise her annoyance. "You concentrate on business and I'll manage strategic planning and operations. Recruitment is my department – with Geoff's assistance. As it happens, the boy in question was an ideal choice. Geoff didn't think so, but he hates kids at the best of times. In fact, I'm tempted to use Barney again. He has a talent for upsetting people, which causes a perfect diversion as far as we're concerned."

"Some youngsters can be smart. Too smart."

"Don't worry. He didn't have a clue what was going on. Although I say it myself, my acting was excellent. It wasn't so much my American voice that was impressive, but the way I stayed friendly and reasonably polite till the end. That's a real struggle for me."

"Quite. You're not known for pulling your punches, Jan. Just make sure that boy doesn't give us any trouble. I don't want MI5 getting a whiff of anything." He unbuttoned his coat and stared up at the vast stained-glass window. "This Barney: can he really be trusted?"

The sun shone through a kaleidoscope of stained glass and dappled their faces in dancing coloured light. "Don't worry," she repeated, but now more assertively. "One sniff of trouble and we'll kill him in an instant. No questions asked."

Chapter 10

"I'm very sorry," Mrs Peters said smugly. "You're too late, Barney. My Disneyland Paris weekend is always oversubscribed and you've missed the boat. I've already got several on the waiting list. Maybe this is a useful learning curve for you. Be quicker to impress your father and keep him on your side, eh? Never mind, there's always next year – or maybe my ski trip. After all, Laura has expressed an interest in that one as well."

Barney was furious. A lot of his friends were going to Disneyland Paris and now he'd have to stay at home on his own. Laura gave him a hug and said how it wouldn't be the same without him. "I only signed up to go because I thought you'd be going, Barney. But cheer up, it's not the end of the world. There's always the ski trip."

"As if my dad will pay for me to go on that," Barney sulked. "He says he's always broke because he has to pay my mum every month. It might help if they actually spoke to each other." He went very quiet before adding awkwardly, "To be honest, I think it's my fault they split up in the first place."

"Don't be silly, Barney. That's just not true. Whatever gave you that idea?"

He looked down uncomfortably. "Mum's a bit stressy at the moment. She's seeing this man from work who's a right muppet. Last night I told her what I thought of him and she got all stroppy and said lots of stuff. We both got upset so things aren't good at the moment. I can't talk to Dad about it – or anything for that matter. Let's face it, he's always telling me what a big disappointment I am to him. Only Gran understands how it is but I don't like to bother her with all my moans."

"You've always got me." Laura squeezed his arm. "I'm a good listener. One day your mum and dad will realise what a clever little Barney they've got!"

"Yeah, yeah, yeah. As if. The only thing I'm good at is annoying everyone. Especially Mrs Peters. I know she hates me."

Laura ruffled his hair. "That's just not true and you know it. Even she likes you sometimes. You've got loads of good points. You're funny and clever and… brilliant at that gym stuff… and I think you're lovely, anyway!"

Despite Laura's reassurances, Barney didn't cheer up all day. There was a lot to think about, especially when a confusing text arrived from an unknown number. All it said was:

```
Don't tell parents about Disneyland
Paris. You will still be going away
somewhere else. You will hear more
soon.
```

But the other strange thing about the message was how it just disappeared. When he tried to read it again, it had been wiped clean.

Walking home from school, Barney called at the newsagents to buy a packet of chocolate raisins. As he came out, biting off the end of the wrapper, a black Volkswagen drew up at the kerb and the woman driver called over to him.

"Excuse me, can you tell me where the park is?"

Barney couldn't help thinking that if she took off those sunglasses behind the dark tinted windows she might be able to see it more clearly.

"Yeah, sure…" He walked over to her and pointed up the street. "You need to go up the hill and turn right at the top…"

She spoke with urgency. "Make sure you're at the school gates to wave off the Disneyland Paris trip. Bring a bag for the weekend. You'll arrive back at the same time as the coach on Sunday."

With a rev of the engine and a spin of the tyres, she'd gone – leaving Barney staring in puzzlement at the smoky dot disappearing over the hill. He was so absorbed in making sense of it all that he was oblivious to the trail of chocolate raisins he'd left behind him.

When he arrived home, another text confirmed he would be attending a training weekend for JRs, but he was forbidden to tell anyone. He wondered what the weekend would involve. Maybe he'd have to drive an Aston Martin around hairpin bends before a bout of martial arts or target practice with a Beretta handgun while dangling from a helicopter. It could be even better than Disneyland Paris, especially without Mrs Peters to nag him day and night.

As far as everyone at school was concerned, Barney was at the school gates to wave off the coach, with

Laura blowing him kisses through the window and Mrs Peters smiling haughtily over her clipboard. Everyone assumed the holdall at Barney's feet was for another weekend trip up to Glasgow. But as far as his parents were concerned, Barney was off to Disneyland Paris. Only Barney and MI5 knew differently.

As soon as the coach pulled away from the school gates, with a cheer from those waving it off, a taxi pulled up. The driver looked at a notepad and called from the window.

"I've come for a… Barney Jones."

Barney climbed in and slid across the back seat as the taxi whisked him away to who knew where? It seemed the driver didn't know where, either. "Where to, sunshine?"

A shrill squeal came from Barney's phone but the driver didn't hear it. It was the teenbuzz ring-tone he'd downloaded. Maybe it was a call from Laura saying she was missing him already. Instead it was a text of meaningless letters and numbers.

"Hold on a minute," Barney called to the driver. "I think I've got a postcode here for your sat nav. Try putting this in…" He read out the numbers as the driver tapped them in, before looking back with a grin. "That's got it, son. Nice little drive ahead. Sit back with your iPod and relax…"

Two hours later, the taxi turned off the road and went through a set of huge iron gates that Barney watched close automatically behind them. Ahead stretched a tree-lined driveway through parkland with sheep and deer grazing under ancient sprawling oaks. Eventually they arrived at a gravelled courtyard in front of an imposing Georgian mansion where the taxi crunched to a halt between two towering stone pillars. The creamy sandstone of the three-story frontage shone bronze in the dying amber sunlight.

"Very nice, too," the driver exclaimed. "I'll be picking you up from here on Sunday at four. Don't get up to mischief, now!"

Barney stepped out of the taxi, clutching his holdall as he looked up apprehensively at the rows of large windows, one of which framed a face peering down at him, before it quickly disappeared.

"Ah, Master Jones," a refined voice called from the top step of the grand entrance. "Do follow me up the stairs. I'll show you to your room and then you can join us for a spot of supper. All the others are here – in the games room, I believe." The man was middle-aged with slicked-back brown hair, wearing a yellow silk neckerchief and tweed sports jacket. *Not like a butler you see in films*, Barney thought. *Very posh, though*.

Two floors up the sweeping spiral staircase with its ornate iron banisters, the man led Barney along a corridor to a large door. He tapped and opened it.

"It's a huge room that sleeps half a dozen but there'll just be the two of you in here."

It was, indeed, a large room with many sash windows looking out into the darkening evening, but the space was divided into bays with wooden partitions and curtains.

"Choose whichever bed you like, apart from the one in the corner. I'll leave you to wash and brush-up and I'll pop back in ten minutes to take you to the dining room."

"Can you just tell me something? Why am I here? I mean, what's going on exactly?"

The man looked horrified. "My dear boy, if you're in the intelligence business then you need to be more subtle than that!" With a sharp snort he turned and left, closing the door behind him.

Barney went to a window and looked down on the courtyard. This was the same window he'd looked up at from the taxi, where there had been a face.

"My dear boy, you need to be more subtle than that!" A gruff voice and giggle came from the corner behind a curtain. Barney couldn't believe his eyes. Poking up like a puppet from behind a partition was a face. A face he knew.

"Blimey, it's you, Seb!"

"How do you do, Barney, my little chum?" With an effortless leap, he swung over the screen, landed elegantly in front of Barney and offered his hand. "You obviously impressed them at the airport. Not that it was one of my better jobs. Still, welcome aboard."

"But…" Barney was speechless, shaking his hand.

"My hair? Yeah, I've had it mown."

"But your voice…"

"Oh that! I used an accent before. Impressed? They teach you how to do all sorts of cool disguises here. It was their idea I wore those dreadful tartan shorts. Anyway, what do you think of the room? I told them we could share. Hope you don't mind. You'd better not snore, though."

"No, but I talk in my sleep. That's the only way you'll get my secrets!" Barney put his bag on a bed before turning back to ask, "Seb, what's happening this weekend? What will we be doing exactly?"

Seb tapped his nose and winked. "Assessment. They'll be weighing us up to see what we can do. Or in your case, how useless you are." He chuckled as he grabbed a pillow and hurled it, hitting Barney full in the face and knocking him back sprawling over his bag.

The pillow fight was getting into full swing when a knock at the door sent both of them scurrying. Within minutes they'd been led down the staircase and into an oak-panelled dining room with one long table in the middle and a row of antique dining chairs on each side. All but two were already occupied by a motley array of teenagers, all of whom were much older than Barney. He looked around, slightly unnerved. They were each involved in whispered conversations and took little notice of Barney as he sat down sheepishly opposite Seb. A few nodded to Seb, but the whole atmosphere was very orderly and subdued, nothing like the noisy dining room at school. At another smaller table at the far end of the room sat four middle-aged men, all dressed in suits. They, too, were intently absorbed in mumbled deliberations.

Following the meal, in which everyone ate in hushed tones, with only the clinking of cutlery to break long periods of silence, one of the men-in-suits announced that all were to attend a meeting in the drawing room in fifteen minutes precisely. Looking at the intense expressions on the faces around him, Barney realised he was well out of his depth. He was by far the youngest in the room and feeling more uncomfortable by the minute. *They're all boffins*, he thought. *It's like being on* University Challenge *and I don't know a thing*. Although Seb was something of a lifeline, even he had become very serious, being engaged in a discussion about the politics of Burma with a boy whose face seemed to be a battlefield of designer stubble and acne. The zits, Barney thought, currently had the upper hand – with a novel's worth of Braille on his chin alone.

When all were gathered in the drawing room, sitting in regimented rows facing a screen, an expectant hush descended long before a balding man in glasses with a clipped moustache appeared at the front. Barney couldn't help thinking he was like a sergeant major addressing his troops before battle. *What on earth have I got myself into?* Barney thought. *There's no way I can get out of this now.*

"Now I suppose many of you know why you are here. Even if you don't, you will have deduced by now, no doubt. Indeed, deduction, observation and surveillance are the themes of this weekend. You will be learning those skills while we –" he paused to look over his glasses at his colleagues – "will be observing and making judgements about all of you." Barney squirmed in his seat. He'd soon be exposed as a fraud or a total failure, before suffering the shame of public ridicule.

The speaker stepped forward, scanned the rows of young faces, then paced up and down the room, ensuring everyone made eye contact, one at a time. It was altogether unnerving and despite being desperate to look away, Barney fixed his eyes on the man's moustache and prayed he wouldn't get asked a question.

"Many are called to attend our assessment programmes, but few are chosen," he went on. "Each of you has been brought here this weekend but no one knows you are here. Should any of you happen to expire in the next forty-eight hours –" he paused again for humorous effect but no one dared to smile – "then, of course, your nearest and dearest will never know. In short, everything that happens here is top secret. This weekend and this place do not exist."

Puzzled looks all round. One girl was taking notes but her pen came to a sudden halt. The man gripped his lapels, sucked in a particularly long breath and continued.

"Should you ever return here, for any reason, there will be no evidence that any of us have ever been. This is not a government establishment. This is normally a health spa and retreat centre which the Ministry has hired for this weekend only. When we all depart on Sunday, the slate will be wiped clean, so to speak. Needless to say, your mobiles will not receive a signal while you are here on account of a temporary blackout. We've also blocked the wi-fi, so no emails. Some of you doubtless depend far too much on the internet, with all your Tweeting, Skyping and blabbing to friends on Facebook. This weekend is about developing real skills; skills which can save your life. I'm sure I needn't warn you that anyone caught disobeying any of these rules will be –" he paused dramatically before adding with relish – "dealt with severely."

He stepped back to consult a note on the table. "While you are here, you are at liberty to wander around the beautiful grounds. You may walk down by the river but do not be tempted to row or swim across just to prove your escapology skills." Nervous giggles. "Also, keep away from the private chapel through the woods. Forbidden territory." He sipped from a glass of water.

Barney shuffled uneasily in his seat. *Disneyland Paris would be far more exciting*, he thought.

"You are all here because of your abilities. Most of you are very bright, speak many languages, possess photographic memories or have a specific skill of use to us – or, should I say, to international security".

So why am I here? Barney wondered. *I can't do anything!*

"I need not tell you that we are not here to play at James Bond fiction, but to make a difference in the real world with its many growing threats…"

The longer the lecture lasted, the more Barney wished he was somewhere else, like on the coach to Paris, sharing sweets with Laura and telling jokes. He didn't belong here and the people around him were a world away from anything he knew. Even Seb sat nodding away, seemingly enthralled.

Just when the man sat down and Barney thought that at last it was time to get out and explore, a girl in the front row walked to a baby grand piano and began a recital, to which they all had to listen intently, giving polite applause between each dull piece.

Climbing the staircase afterwards, everyone discussed pretentiously the finer points of the Beethoven piano sonata .

"Do you play?" someone asked Barney.

"Yeah, quite a bit. Rugby, mostly." He got a stony response and an icy stare.

"I'm something of a rugger man myself," the spotty-faced boy joined in. "I've had trials for England but from the sound of you," he sneered, "you're more of a Wales chap."

Barney grinned. "And proud of it."

A gangly boy in a yellow waistcoat chipped in. "Actually, chess is much more my thing for relaxation. What do you do to relax your mind?" he asked.

"Sleep normally does the trick," Barney said, before adding for dramatic effect, "or illegal substances." There were horrified looks all round.

When they were alone in their room, Seb stood by an open window, which he pointed at with one hand while beckoning to Barney with the other. He then held up a notepad and wrote:

'Climb out. Can't talk in here. Most likely bugged.'

Barney leaned out of the window and looked down. It didn't look too much of a problem, with enough of a ledge and a drainpipe not far off to make scrambling down and climbing back again relatively easy. After all, his expertise on the climbing wall at school never failed to impress everyone at gym club. He turned back, gave the thumbs up and slithered out onto the ledge. The night was cold and the moon was already peeping through the clouds.

With his face pressed against the wall and his fingertips gripping every groove, Barney edged his way along the front of the house, towards the drainpipe. Seb was just behind, muttering how a Spiderman suit should be standard kit for to all JRs. On reaching the pipe, Barney wrapped his limbs around it and clambered down onto the gravel courtyard. Seb crunched beside him before they scurried off into the shadows to disappear in the shrubbery. Squatting behind a clipped box hedge, Seb tugged at Barney's leg.

"Down here. We can talk here. Just beware that even the walls have ears."

Barney sat with his knees to his chest and sulked. "I could have been at Disneyland Paris tonight."

"Listen, Barney. I'm sorry. I hope you don't have any hard feelings about me investigating you on the plane. I thought you were a good kid and I told them so. I'm glad they think you're sound and want to use you. It's just that…" He paused for a long time.

"What?"

"You need to be careful. I can't say much but I'm aware something big is happening. It must be serious because you got to meet the boss at the airport. She's known as Aries. Quite formidable, by all accounts. MI5 are clearly rattled by what they found out from you. You realise there's a major terrorist threat at the moment? It's an organisation called Korova – planning to attack soft military targets, it seems. Just watch your back, that's all. If Korova gets wind you're involved with all this business, they're sure to be after you. Ruthless, they are. I know of two JRs who've disappeared without trace. Both of them were doing low-key surveillance on Korova. It's a tough business we're in and I thought I'd better warn you about what you're letting yourself in for. It seems some of Korova already know you. So take care, Barney. I wouldn't want you to be number three to go missing."

Barney was quiet for some time, Seb's chilling words sending a shiver right through him. He tried to make light of this sudden bolt from the blue. "Thanks, Seb. I didn't know you cared! Anyway, how did you get into this spying lark?"

"Like most of them in there tonight – it's in the family. Connections. My father works for the Diplomatic Service and recommended me. To be fair, the money comes in handy as I'm planning to go to Edinburgh University next year. Most of us here this weekend are being groomed to be spies at university. You'd be surprised how many files MI5 keeps on student fanatics and hot-heads. That kind of work doesn't bother me. It's just this Korova stuff that's scary. They're a callous bunch of extremists that will stop at nothing."

Barney fell silent again before asking pensively, "So if that woman on the plane, the one with the eyebrow ring, is one of these Korova extremists, why did she want to kidnap me? My dad wouldn't pay them any ransom money to get me back. He'd probably pay them to keep me!"

"They probably want to brainwash a few kids to work for them. You obviously looked like a suitable recruit." Seb grinned before adding, "They can't have very high standards, can they?"

Suddenly a glare of lights swept past them and they heard tyres on gravel. Peeping out from the hedge, they saw a large shiny black car pulling up at the house. There was enough light to see the woman step out of the car and shake the hand of one of the men in suits. She was short, wore a suit and looked familiar. She was none other than the woman he'd faced across the desk at the airport.

"It's her," Barney said. "She who must be obeyed. The one you called Aries."

Seb whistled softly. "Wow. You know what that means. Something mega-serious is afoot."

CHAPTER 11

Breakfast at the long table was even more dismal than the dreary meal the night before when hardly anyone spoke. *Nothing like the fun and laughs at Disneyland Paris*, Barney thought.

"It's a bundle of fun this morning," he grunted to a serious face in front of him.

"We're not here to play childish games," the boy scoffed. "To be honest, I'm surprised they let a kid like you come here in the first place. It doesn't take a genius to see you're not exactly top-drawer material."

Barney stared at the boy's distorted nose with its unsymmetrical nostrils. "There's no need to be toffee-nosed about it." He grinned. "Talking of childish games, it looks like you might play a few yourself. Boxing, by any chance?" He mimicked the boy's snobbish tone. "Has one had a spot of fisticuffs before breakfast, one wonders?"

The boy's eyes flashed like blades and his cut-glass voice cracked. "I can't think why they've brought a common little Welsh squirt here. It so lowers the tone."

"Aries happens to think I'm cute," Barney carried on, determined to wind him up further.

"Cute?" he mocked. "Like an incontinent piglet with a slobbering snout."

"Really?" Barney couldn't resist a quick shot across the bows. "You're obviously something of an expert on noses. And I can tell I'm really getting up yours. Well, let's face it, there's certainly room!"

The boy's fists clenched and a bubble of milky saliva spilled over his bottom lip, carrying with it a stray Rice Krispie. His left eye quivered as the rage rose in his throat and the expletives spilled out. "I could kill you with my bare hands," he growled.

"No need," Barney chirped, "you're already doing it with your face."

A Rice Krispie spat across the table and hit Barney in the eye. "Oh no," he exclaimed melodramatically, "I've been shot by a… wait for it… a cereal killer!"

The girl next to the boy snorted and guffawed like a horse. "Oh Tarquin, you must admit he's an absolute hoot!"

"I will not be humiliated by a snivelling little upstart," Tarquin seethed. "So he'd better watch out." He stood up, pushed his cereal bowl across the table and stomped off like a spoilt child, as milk pebbled with Rice Krispies slopped across the polished surface.

"Don't worry about Tarquin," the girl said. "He's a bit touchy this morning. He was dumped by his girlfriend last night. Highly-strung, if you ask me."

Barney said nothing and reached for the muesli. He could only sigh with disappointment at the thought of all the lively breakfast banter at Disneyland Paris. He took out his phone to send Laura a text but the girl opposite stared disapprovingly.

"You might just as well put that away for the weekend. Weren't you listening last night? They've blocked all signals. We're a communication-free zone. The outside world can't get to us here. A good job, too, if you ask me."

"So what exactly have they got in store for us today?" Barney muttered, returning his phone to his pocket.

"Workshops," she said, blowing the steam from her coffee cup. "You need to sign up on the board at reception. If I were you, I'd keep out of Tarquin's way. He's known to harbour grudges for months."

"Then I'd better go and see what's on offer – the excitement's killing me." Barney took his empty bowl to a trolley.

"There's a two-hour lunch break," the girl called after him. "Tarquin will doubtless be mooching about in the library. Probably best if you stick to the riverside walk, out of harm's way. That's my advice."

Barney shrugged. "I'm certainly not bothered about him." He walked out through the reception area, signed the board for a couple of workshops that seemed the least boring, then ran up the grand spiral staircase. As he reached the top, a face came into view. A face with a familiar nose and a look of sneering contempt. Tarquin's eyes smouldered with rage – he'd clearly been waiting in ambush. No one else was on the stairs or on the landing beyond. He stepped forward as Barney bounced up the last few steps.

"I've been waiting for you, kid."

"You didn't finish your Rice Krispies," Barney panted. "You won't grow into a strong boy."

Tarquin said nothing as he clenched his teeth and his fist. Barney jumped onto the top step as Tarquin lunged at him, his fist flying. Instinctively, Barney ducked and dived away from the banister, to avoid plunging over the top and hurtling into space. He followed through the manoeuvre with an elegant spring onto his feet on the landing. By the time Barney performed a finishing bow with a satisfied smile, Tarquin had already launched himself off the top step, having made a serious misjudgement. His plan had depended on his fist slamming into Barney's face to stop him losing balance and tumbling forward. With the full force of his punch missing its target, Tarquin sprawled headfirst down the stairs, nose-diving onto the sixth step and plunging down the stairway with a gurgling grunt. Head-butting the tenth step, his lip split open and he spat blood, flecked with soggy Rice Krispies. By the time he slammed into the banister, snapping his collar bone like a brittle twig, he was screaming. It was only as he wedged his foot through the banister on the next bend, twisting his ankle and scraping his shin, that he spread-eagled to an undignified halt halfway round the second curve of the stairs. He lay on his back, spluttering obscenities through frothing, bloody teeth as Barney casually glanced down with a shrug. "One way to straighten your nose!"

He turned with a chuckle and returned to his bedroom, where he delighted in telling Seb about the whole incident.

"That's terrible," Seb said. "No one upsets Tarquin. He's the son of the Home Secretary."

"In that case, he should know better. It was an unprovoked attack. Well, slightly unprovoked. I didn't lay a finger on him. His wounds are all self-inflicted. Helped by just a bit of gravity, that's all."

Seb stifled a snigger. "Just hope Aries doesn't get to hear about it. She works with the Home Secretary."

Barney grinned. "Look at me, Seb. Do I look bothered?"

"Even so, I think we'd better keep clear of Tarquin for the rest of today. How about exploring the grounds at lunchtime? We could have a bit of fun. Meet me down by the boathouse."

The lunch break was a long time coming. Barney kept looking at his watch during a particularly long talk by an anti-terrorist trainer and a Powerpoint presentation on the latest electronic surveillance kit. He was aware of people giving him sideways glances and disapproving stares. Clearly the news of Tarquin's downfall had spread and Barney was viewed with a mixture of suspicion and disgrace – nothing like the hero he thought he'd be. It was good to get out at last and to head down to the river to find Seb.

The wide sweep of the river meandered lazily around the lower lawns and ornamental gardens. Barney stared into the sliding soupy water. *A bit like the sludgy oxtail soup at lunch,* he thought, before he headed towards the boathouse to shelter from the drizzle carried by a blustery wind.

"How's the Tarquin Tormentor?" Seb was stooping in the doorway, dragging on a cigarette.

Barney hunched his shoulders against the wind. "Just think, I could be hurtling round on a roller coaster with all my mates right now. Present company excepted, this is the pits."

"His arm's in a sling and he's lost a tooth. You've certainly made your mark, Barney! You're a breath of fresh air to all this business. I hope they put us on a job together."

Barney peered through the slats of the boathouse doors, the murky water slapping at its supports. "Fancy rowing across?" he said mischievously. "There are a few canoes in there. Who's to know? And if they do, who cares? I'm obviously in trouble as it is, so a bit more can't hurt."

Seb threw his cigarette into the reeds. "Better still – you see that long canvas bag with the aluminium tubes poking out? That's a hang glider. I've had a few lessons. Fancy a spin?"

"Where from?" Barney asked, his eyes already flashing. "I thought you had to throw yourself off a cliff with those things."

Seb was already squeezing into the dark interior of the boathouse. "Not if you know how to get decent lift. Easy in this wind. Besides, I've got a good idea where we can jump from."

They dragged the frame, its sails and harness from its shelf. "I can soon assemble this and fit the battens and we'll have the ultimate flying machine!" Seb announced proudly. "Grab the end and follow me."

He led Barney through a clump of trees and climbed a hill to where a small ivy-clad church tower stood overlooking miles of parkland. Seb pushed open a door and led the way up dark, damp, twisting stone steps.

Eventually they emerged into the open at the top of the tower, overlooking the entire estate, with the river now just a glinting snake beyond the trees.

Seb took a deep breath, surveyed the scene and barked his orders like a wing commander. "I'll go first to show you what to do, then it's your turn. We'll need to jump off this side of the tower into the wind and our aim is to land in the middle of that field of cows in the distance."

"That's miles away!" Barney was both excited and petrified.

"No problem," Seb said calmly as he stretched out the wings, fitted them into place and attached various wires. "The objective is always to stay airborne in the uplifting currents of air. You soon develop an eye for a good thermal and simply ride it. You'll find it absolutely exhilarating. This is the harness that hangs under the wings by these straps. You just slip inside after leaping off the wall and lie face-down to enjoy the ride. You control everything by shifting your body weight. Lean to the right and the right wing dips and slows, thus turning the whole caboodle. To go faster you move forward, pulling yourself further in front of this control bar; to slow down, backwards. Nothing to it. Watch me and you'll soon get the hang of it. Ha – get it? The *hang* of it!"

Barney squinted into the breeze as Seb barked further instructions. "Whatever you do, don't cross the river. There's an army of pylons and dirty great overhead wires. Not only will you black out half the country, you'll be instant toast." He called over his shoulder as he balanced on the wall, clutching the cross-bar. "Just watch me. Take-off is the tricky bit. After that it's plain sailing. Grip this control bar, leap off and throw back your legs into the harness, just like this…"

With a cry of "Geronimo!" Seb was airborne – not swooping to the ground but amazingly hovering overhead for a few seconds, before gliding majestically in a straight flight path, occasionally climbing and seeming to hang motionless in mid-air. Barney watched him wheeling like a buzzard above the main drive before banking round gracefully to head into the cow field. Now, no more than a dragonfly in the distance, the glider descended into what appeared a gentle perfect landing.

Barney's adrenaline was already racing. What a fantastic ride – it could even beat Disneyland Paris. He waited, pacing up and down, as Seb trudged his way back to the tower. At last he emerged at the top of the steps with a beaming smile and jeans spattered with cow dung.

It didn't take long for Barney to be eagerly poised, his toes over the edge of the wall and his hands gripping the bar, with the canopy stretching above him.

"The secret is to stay calm and not to move suddenly," Seb commanded. "Just think you're a bird, that the wings are your own and the sky is all yours. Best of luck."

Barney leaned forward, took a deep breath as if he was about to leap off a diving board, hurled himself from the tower and braced himself for a rapid descent. Instead, he found himself floating in mid-air, peering down at the ground moving far below. He pushed his legs further back into the harness, grasping the control bar with outstretched arms, and felt the air fill the wings. He gasped with the sheer thrill of soaring like an eagle. He moved his body, gripping so tightly that his knuckles whitened, as he felt every slight response from the wings. The wind rushed at his face as he swerved to the left, then shifted his weight to correct himself, then banked sharply, heading towards the front of the house. Each time he tried to correct himself, the frame seemed to twist and over-respond, sending him swirling one way and then another. No longer able to enjoy the view from a graceful glide, he dipped into an abrupt spin. Pulling for all he was worth to lift the nose, he slowed slightly but a sudden gust buffeted the canopy, upset his balance and sent him into a spiralling nose-dive.

Nothing Barney did brought any response as he hurtled towards the main drive. He tried to release his legs to break his fall as he plummeted ever faster. As he pulled and twisted in the hope of steering away from the hard surface of the drive, he veered straight towards a car pulling away from the courtyard – a shiny black Daimler. There was nothing he could do to avoid colliding, so he kicked out his feet and braced himself for impact. Skimming across the bonnet, his knee cracking the windscreen, he clattered over the roof before cart-wheeling down the other side. The crossbar scraped across the gleaming paintwork and gouged a jagged groove over the boot, before wedging in the rear bumper as the car slammed to a halt in a spray of gravel. Buckled poles and crumpled sails crunched onto the drive, just as everything happened at once: the rip of a gunshot, the burst of a front tyre and the screech of a siren blasting from under the bonnet. Armed guards suddenly appeared from nowhere, shouting and commanding Barney to 'freeze', their machine guns raised, dogs barking and straining at their handlers' rattling chains. Stunned and bruised though he was, Barney was wrenched violently to his feet and swiftly frogmarched into the house. Dragged down steps into a small cellar, he was manhandled, frisked and made to stand with his hands on the wall above his head. Words like 'imposter', 'double agent' and 'Korova attack' were bandied around until the door opened, a short woman in a suit entered and all fell silent.

"None of those," she snapped. "A childish prank. My fault. I took a risk with this one. I should have followed my better judgment. Leave me alone with him. Just five minutes."

As the men hurriedly left the room, Aries pushed a chair towards Barney.

"Sit down."

"I'm sorry," he muttered, unable to look her in the eye. "About the car. I didn't think…"

"Exactly. You didn't think. You're an immature fool."

This time Barney looked up. He couldn't leave her unchallenged. "I'm much younger than everyone else here. I'm only thirteen. I make mistakes."

"We can't afford to make mistakes in this business," she snapped. "But it seems I made one with you. I should have realised you're not in the same league as the others. After all, your background isn't exactly top quality, is it? Not like the others here."

Her words struck Barney like a blow to the head. The one thing that riled him was being considered inferior because of his parents or of where he lived. He glared at her with mounting rage.

"My background has got nothing to do with it. I'm younger, that's all. I'm entitled to make mistakes – it's called learning."

"Don't try to be clever. You're not. You let me down and I don't suffer fools gladly. Firstly, I'm told you climbed out of your room last night on some childish caper…"

"That's what children do."

"Be quiet. Secondly, you seriously injured another JR who required hospital treatment." She stood directly in front of him, glaring down with a searing stare that burned right through him.

"Tarquin tried to—"

She stamped her foot. "Don't interrupt me."

He looked up at her, startled, but growing even more annoyed. "Tarquin deserved everything he got."

"And now you do this brainless prank. Had the in-car radar sensed you any sooner, you'd have been shot down as a potential suicide bomber."

"Or a kamikaze hang-glider pilot." His sarcasm was designed to annoy her. He wasn't prepared to sit there and be nagged like this. No one ever listened to him and it delighted him to know he was making such an important figure lose control.

"This is far from a joking matter and clearly demonstrates that you just cannot be trusted or relied upon. One of our marksmen had you in his sights just before you hit the ground. You were very lucky his bullet hit the tyre and not you. It was altogether totally mindless. So, tell me straight – was Seb involved in this stupid antic as well?"

Barney paused. "You just said you don't trust me. So whatever I answer, you're not likely to believe me." He wasn't prepared to land Seb in trouble.

"I repeat, was Seb involved?" She was becoming even more agitated. It felt like one of his sessions of winding up Mrs Peters at school.

"Whether I falsely accuse him or lie to protect him, aren't you giving an untrustworthy person the power to mislead you? Is that wise?"

She screamed, "How dare you speak to me like this! I have never met such—"

"Attitude?"

She fixed her piercing glare on Barney for a few more seconds before she had to look away, her face unable to hide her fury. Inwardly he was still angry at the way he was being treated but he felt great satisfaction that he was able to act calmly while she was clearly getting increasingly rattled.

"Attitude," he went on, "is what they accuse me of when I'm annoying. Truth often annoys adults. Like with Tarquin…"

"I don't wish to discuss Tarquin."

Barney rubbed his knee. It was throbbing from when he'd slammed into the windscreen. "I thought I might have the right to tell my side of the story. The truth."

"No." She scowled. "You have no rights now. You will remain in this room by yourself until your taxi arrives tomorrow. You will tell no one of what has happened.

You will tell no one of this weekend or of this incident. It never happened. You will be returned and removed from our database. Never cross my path again. You are of no use to us."

"We'll see."

Barney couldn't believe his bravado. He knew his attitude was getting out of order but this woman annoyed him and he couldn't stop himself now. After all, she couldn't be any more formidable or vicious than Mrs Peters in one of her moods. He looked up, folded his arms and smiled. It was the last straw. She swore and stormed from the room.

In the cool silence, Barney examined the bruise on his knee and contemplated his twenty-four hour solitary confinement. This was nothing like the fun at Disneyland Paris but at last he felt strangely satisfied. After all, he'd almost mastered flight, he'd almost killed the Home Secretary's son and he'd almost given the head of MI5 a coronary. He felt ashamed of such an appalling attitude; but on the other hand, he had to smile. Not bad for half a day's work.

CHAPTER 12

FEBRUARY, THE ALBERT MEMORIAL, HYDE PARK, LONDON

The brigadier climbed the steps sedately and glanced down self-importantly at people walking in the park, before bending to examine the carved figures around the base of the monument. He rose, straight-backed, to peer up at the golden statue of Prince Albert bathed in watery sunlight.

"Quite hideous, ostentatious Victoriana. Nonetheless, somehow admirable." He spoke only to himself and the pigeons perched at Albert's feet. He raised his arm and pulled back his sleeve; a diamond-studded cufflink caught the wintry sun. As footsteps approached, he turned slowly to glance down at the running figure squinting up at him.

"You're late," the brigadier barked. "By fifty-two seconds precisely."

"Sorry, sir. Bit of a hold-up at South Kensington." The gruff voice seemed a mixture of accents, with significant American influences.

"Punctuality is crucial. I thought you'd know that, being military-trained."

"Only too well, sir."

"I recruited you on Geoff's recommendation. He informs me you are very professional when it comes to…" He looked around to make sure they were totally alone. "When it comes to explosives."

"Absolutely, sir."

"I think we should walk." He led the way back down the steps and they headed through the park, suspending their conversation whenever a jogger approached.

"We'll walk to a splendid bronze statue in Kensington Gardens, of my friend Jenner."

"How's the operation going so far, sir?" the black-haired man with the permanent squint and pockmarked face asked enthusiastically.

"That's what I want to see you about. It's six months to J1. My side of things is good. I want you to head-up J2. That's in nine months, just over the road there." He pointed at the famous domed building across the street. "I'll pay you double. I've already got Korova members on the staff there at the Royal Albert Hall. It should make your preparation work much easier. They'll tell you where all the CCTV cameras are installed. It's vital you're not seen on any of them. If your cover is blown, I'll cancel all subsequent payments. I've chosen you because, like me, you've served time behind bars and, according to Geoff, you're ruthless, efficient and, also like me, bitter. Both of us have old scores to settle. I don't want anyone to know what's hit them until it's too late."

The man tried to smile but it didn't come naturally. "It will be my honour, sir. Trust me."

The brigadier casually glanced up at a squirrel scampering through bare branches. "I trust no one."

Behind them Prince Albert continued to look down disapprovingly, but powerless to prevent the sinister plot unfolding before his golden eyes.

Chapter 13

Mrs Peters sat in her classroom, sipping a mug of coffee with 'I Love My Teacher' emblazoned across it.

"To be honest, Barnaby, I'm putting your application for the ski trip on hold until I discuss things with your father. Since you missed Disneyland Paris you've been particularly difficult and rather full of yourself. I thought missing the trip might have sharpened up your attitude but it seems it's the reverse. You've taken a dive, I'm afraid."

"Are you open to bribery and corruption, miss?"

"You see, this demonstrates my point. To you, your silly comments are funny. To the rest of us, you're nothing but irritating. We can only tolerate so much of your annoying and immature remarks. Why are you looking at me like that?"

"Like what? This is how I always look!"

"Barnaby, it's quite normal for teenagers to want to test the system, to kick against authority or to think they know it all. But at least most of them give it a rest now and again. Do me a favour and give your attitude a little holiday – a well-deserved break. How about a gap year? Send it backpacking around the world!"

She gave a satisfied smirk, gathered an armful of books and swept from the room. Barney went to find Laura to console him in his hour of need.

"Don't worry, Barney. We'll work on her. Treat it as a challenge." She smiled and gave him a quick hug. He so wanted to tell her about his disastrous episode at 'spy school' but knew he was strictly sworn to secrecy.

"You're just on a bit of a downer at the minute." Laura smiled reassuringly. "But you trampoliners always bounce back!"

The trampoline was Barney's only crumb of comfort. A few more trophies and a successful public display helped restore a modicum of pride. Then Mr Cheng, who ran the gym club, made an offer Barney couldn't refuse.

"How do you fancy a challenge, Barney? I'm taking a squad to enter a gym tournament in London. It'll be in front of a massive crowd at the Royal Albert Hall. A great experience for you, competing against the best in your league. What d'you think?"

Barney was stunned. "Me? But I'm the youngest in the team. It would be awesome but am I good enough for something so epic?"

"I wouldn't ask you if I didn't have faith in you, Barney. I don't just think you're a good gymnast; I think you're a sound, reliable lad. Despite what some staff might say about you, I think your attitude and determination are just what we need in the team. You won't get another chance like this. It'll be a great challenge."

"Count me in, sir. I'm always up for anything scary!"

This was an opportunity, Barney felt sure, for him to prove himself once and for all. Whatever the result, he hoped Mrs Peters would give him some respect for having a go.

Laura was more than impressed. "Wow, Barney – the Royal Albert Hall is amazing. I'm dead proud of you!"

The following weeks were filled with rigorous training. Mr Cheng kept up the pressure to make sure the team reached the highest standard.

"You've all come on in leaps and bounds." He grinned, while everyone groaned. "Seriously, though – I have every confidence in you bringing back a trophy or two from this important event. Barney's been a real star this week, so keep watching his style, particularly with straddle jumps, backward somersaults and crash dives. He'll be doing a solo trampoline routine under spotlights in the middle of the arena and in front of a crowd of thousands. No pressure!"

Everyone cheered as Barney beamed and tingled with anticipation.

As soon as he entered the Royal Albert Hall at midday, Barney and his teammates were bowled over by its size and atmosphere. Having climbed flights of stairs, they breathlessly peered down from the uppermost gallery into the arena, squinting at distant gymnasts already rehearsing their routines for the evening competition. A few competitors were scattered around the vast auditorium, watching from the sea of burgundy seats, while electricians adjusted lights from scaffolding towers. The buzz of activity made no more sound than awed whispers echoing around a cavernous cathedral. Barney looked up at the huge saucers suspended from the ceiling and imagined himself leaping from one to another before somersaulting into a spectacular crash dive to the trampoline in the middle of the arena far below. His fantasy was interrupted by Mr Cheng reading his mind.

"Don't even think of it, Barney. Right, listen up everyone. Our rehearsal session starts on the dot of one-thirty. You're all to be in the arena then for the organisers to measure our timing and finalise the programme. If you're late, you'll miss the boat and be out of the tournament – as well as have me to deal with. Under no circumstances is anyone to go walkabout. Stay right here in the gallery and enjoy the view, while I find out where we eat our sandwiches and get kitted up, and I'll collect you once I've spoken to the powers-that-be." He gave a stern stare before jogging off along the corridor.

Barney checked the time on his cow watch while walking slowly around the gallery, looking down at the rows of seats and imagining the crowds later in the day. Cleaners hoovered in faraway aisles and armies of electricians were fitting cables around the arena. Just below him two men in overalls were in deep discussion. It was only when Barney glanced at them for a second time that he froze. He was just above them, staring down onto the top of their heads. One had thick black hair but the other had a bald patch with a smudgy purple birthmark – just like the shape of Australia.

"It's him. Australia Head," Barney muttered, ducking to peer through the rails at the man's every move. Both men were absorbed in lifting a small hatch in an aisle between seats but Barney had no doubt this was the very same man who'd planted the explosive in his trophy at the airport. What was he doing here? Barney called over to one of his teammates. "I've just got to pop downstairs a minute. I won't be long."

The man below was now recording images on a miniature camera, which he pointed at rows of seats, then at the royal box. Barney knew MI5 wanted this man, so quick action on his part would be vital. It would take some explaining to Mr Cheng but there wasn't time to worry about that now. Australia Head was already walking out into the corridor underneath the gallery. Barney had no idea what he was going to do, but he dashed down the stairs. On the floor below he ran along the corridor that circled the building. There was no sign of Australia Head anywhere and Barney was soon lost. After diving down stairways, through more corridors and eventually completing several circuits, he found himself in a deserted passageway. He crept along it, not knowing what was beyond the door in front of him. He heard a voice on the other side. Taking a deep breath, he pushed it open and ran through – to face a woman sitting alone at a table, giggling into a phone. She wore a badge that said 'Catering'. She mouthed "closed" at him.

"Excuse me," Barney panted. "Can I speak to someone to do with security? It's important."

The woman held up her hand, swivelled in her chair and continued her conversation with her back to him.

"It could be urgent, in fact," Barney added more forcefully.

"Sorry, Saskia," the woman laughed into the phone, "I've got a young man here in a bit of a flap. I'd better go and sort out the little chap. Speak soon, darling, and don't forget what I said about the weekend." She gave a squeal, snorted "Tar-rah" and turned to Barney.

"Now then, young man, what can I do for you? You look a bit stressed."

"I've just seen a man in there who's... well, he's a criminal. He's wanted by the police."

The woman tapped a pen on the table and moved her tongue slowly along her teeth.

"How do you know he's a criminal exactly, darling?"

"I've seen him before. They told me to let them know if I ever see him again."

"They?"

"Security Services – anti-terrorist. The thing is, I think he's planning something here."

She gave a sideways glance and rolled her eyes. "Maybe I'll get one of the temporary security guys to have a chat with you, how's that? And your name is?"

"Barney."

She smiled patronisingly. "Not James Bond, then." She pressed numbers on her phone, eyeing Barney up and down as she did so. Even though she tried to whisper, he detected by the tone in her voice that she wasn't taking him very seriously.

"Hi, Roger. It's Tina. Any chance of you popping over? I've got an interesting one for you. Says it's urgent. A lad called Barney something-or-other."

Barney looked round at a large poster of a poppy. The woman looked up and smiled, as if he'd just popped in for a chat. "That's one of the big events here each year. You may have seen it on TV. Remembrance Day is my favourite – all those soldiers and the royals. Some of the organisers are in today. It takes months of planning."

Barney wasn't interested in small-talk and looked past her into another corridor. She went on, oblivious to his agitation. "So are you here with your school? You like gymnastics?"

He couldn't disguise his growing frustration any longer. "Yes. Look, I'm not making this stuff up. Maybe I should go back and find him myself. Mind you, it could turn nasty after what he said to me last time. In fact, he might even be here to get me. Maybe he found out I was coming here today."

The woman was looking very uneasy. "Not to worry. Roger will soon sort you out."

"Did I hear my name?" A man in a security uniform strode in, rattling keys. "Is this him?" he asked, not even looking at Barney. He held a radio transmitter that fizzed and crackled. Barney's heart sank. This wasn't a burly bouncer who'd soon deal with trouble, but a little man with sunken cheeks, bulgy eyes and a hotchpotch of brown teeth.

"That's him," the woman said, waving her pen at Barney.

The man folded his arms, giving a wry smile. "He looks a bundle of trouble! Right, son, what's your problem?"

"There's a man in there who I happen to know is a member of a terrorist organisation. He didn't see me but there's no way he should be let loose in this place."

"Hey, hey… hold on a moment." The man held up a hand as if stopping the traffic. "Are you trying to tell me my job?"

"Well, you're probably not aware—"

The man stepped forward, in full command. "Do you think I don't know what's going on here? I don't need some kid off the street to come in and make stupid suggestions. Too many computer games and kids' movies, that's the trouble. Ain't that so, Tina?"

He folded his arms again, looking most satisfied with his performance, and gave a smarmy wink at the woman checking orders on her laptop.

"Thanks, Roger. You do it so much better than me." She giggled.

Barney was furious. "So you're dismissing me as a nutter without even checking out what I'm telling you?"

The man paused. "In a word: *yes*. We have a complete record of everyone in the building. You included. You're on CCTV as we speak, so smile nicely. All staff have been thoroughly vetted and bags have been searched. My company takes security seriously and you're quite safe. There, are you reassured now?"

"For all you know," Barney could feel the anger cracking his voice, "I could be a terrorist. I got in here easily, didn't I? Some bloke at the door peered in my sports bag but for all he knew I could have had dangerous stuff concealed in my sandwich box."

"Of course, son. Something like deadly sausage rolls or crisps past their sell-by date?"

"I think you'll find just a small amount of TATP could cause a significant fire bomb." Barney turned to the woman sitting open-mouthed. "That's triacetone triperoxide, in case you wondered."

"Don't try to sound smart with me, son." The man was clearly irritated. "There are regular checks over the entire premises with sniffer dogs and x-ray equipment. You'd soon be rumbled."

"Not if I used some sort of scent-shield. Just like the guy in there uses. Ever heard of Korova?"

For the first time the man seemed lost for words and there was an uneasy silence. The woman pretended to be absorbed in her laptop.

"Right, son. You come inside and point out this evil monster and I shall prove to you just how wrong you are and how efficient our security assessment programme is. I don't see why I should waste my time but if it puts that little mind of yours at rest, then it'll all be worthwhile. It's the price we pay for all these spy DVDs you youngsters watch these days. Everyone thinks there's a baddie round every corner. But not here. That's the beauty of working in a big round building – no corners to hide in, hey, Tina?"

She gave an exaggerated cackle as the man led Barney out through the corridor, down some stairs and into the auditorium. They stood in the arena, with gymnasts bouncing around them, as Barney scanned the tiers of empty seats. Standing under the spotlights, it was difficult to see beyond the front stalls. He cupped his hand over his forehead and squinted upwards.

"Go on then," the man barked. "Show me just where this demon of yours is lurking."

"He was up there." Barney pointed vaguely into the darkness, already aware his efforts were pointless.

The man grunted and sighed. "So you've had your little bit of attention. How about joining your school team and concentrating on what you came here for? You leave security to me and I'll leave bouncing on a trampoline to you. Then we'll all be a lot happier. You do your job and I'll do mine."

He walked away, mumbling to himself about the spoilt brats of today.

Barney was left staring into the void, searching for just a glint of a needle in the haystack of maroon seats, all the way from the organ pipes to the royal box and back again. It was as he narrowed his eyes to peer up at the organ that he was sure he caught sight of the two men high up in the upper gallery. Without thinking twice, he ran for the stairs, snatching his phone from his pocket while leaping two steps at a time. He was determined to get a picture as proof that an undesirable was still in their midst and that he wasn't an attention-seeking little liar.

The upper gallery was empty apart from a single figure at the far end crouching in the semi-darkness. Barney stepped back into the corridor and headed for the next door closest to where the figure was lurking. Creeping through it, he hid behind a pillar from where he could video the man, just metres away. He pointed his phone but it suddenly went off with its ear-splitting high-pitched squawk. Instinctively, he smothered it under his arm to kill the noise, desperately hoping the teenbuzz ring-tone didn't work on large middle-aged men at such close range. Seeing the man was unaware of the noise, Barney scuttled back to the doorway to answer his call. The voice was Mr Cheng's.

"Get here immediately, Jones. I told you not to wander off. To the arena, now."

"Sorry, sir. I've just got to sort something out. Won't be long. The thing is, sir – no I can't speak now. Call me back in a minute."

Before he could stuff the phone in his pocket, a hand snatched it from him. He blinked up at a face he knew, with its mean stare, sweaty upper lip and blotchy double-chin. The jaw moved with the vigorous chewing of gum and once again Barney felt that warm spearmint breath on his face, as a chubby hand grabbed his throat.

"Creeping up on me, eh? Hey, I know your face. I've seen you before."

Barney could hardly speak as the hand tightened at his neck and the only thing he could think to splutter was, "Can I have my phone back, please?"

With his right hand still clenched at Barney's throat, the man single-handedly unbuttoned his chest pocket and stuffed the phone into it before refastening and clenching his fist to strike the back of Barney's head.

Barney gasped. "I'll take that as a no, then."

The next blow sent him sprawling across the corridor before the man's foot crunched on his wrist and pinned him to the floor. "What are you doing here? What do you know?" Each word was pronounced slowly, in a dangerous whisper that finished in a hissing spray of minty spit. "You're that kid from the airport. I didn't like you then and I don't like you now. Who sent you?"

"I'm here with my school. I saw you and I popped up to say hello, that's all."

"Do you take me for a fool?" He bent down to grab Barney's collar. "You've got one minute to tell me all you know. I can snap your neck like a match, so get talking. Try to call for help or raise your voice and it'll be the last thing you ever yelp."

Barney could see past the man's shoulder at the other man emerging through the shadows. His face was sweaty and pockmarked, with a squinty bloodshot eye. He spoke with a gruff foreign accent. "There's a store room just through that door. Take the kid inside and get rid of him. No one will hear you strangle him in there. Be quick."

He took a bundle of flex from a toolbox, wrenched Barney's arms behind his back and tied his wrists tightly. Before Barney could yelp at the pain, a strip of gaffer tape was slapped firmly over his mouth and he was bundled along the corridor to a door marked 'PRIVATE'.

"I'll stay out here while you deal with the kid," Squint-Eye said, as Barney tried to squeal for help. He was desperately trying to think what he could do but his mind was in a whir of panic and rising fear. His struggles were useless and he was swiftly thrown through the door onto a pile of cardboard boxes in a stockroom stacked with chairs, crates of scaffolding and cleaning kit. There were no windows and only a single fluorescent strip-light dangling precariously on a chain from the low ceiling. It spluttered into life with a buzz when Australia Head stretched an arm and thumped the switch, just missing a nail poking out of the wall. He slammed the door behind him and approached Barney, who was still lying face-down on top of a crumpled box in the middle of the room. He grabbed Barney's collar and flipped him onto his back, while grabbing an iron bar to push against his throat.

"Before I delight in smashing your pretty little face in, I'll ask you one more time. Who are you and what do you know?" He ripped the tape from Barney's mouth. "You have just seconds to talk."

Barney winced as the tape tore from his lips. His heart was pounding and his mouth went so dry he could hardly speak. "I'm Barney Jones," he croaked, squinting into the strip light just above him.

"I know. Who sent you?"

"No one." He felt a numbing blow to the side of his head.

"I want the truth." More frothy flecks of spearmint flew.

Barney's mind was racing madly. He'd have to play for time. "All right," he heard himself say. "I'll tell you. I'll tell you everything."

The man relaxed his grip on Barney's shirt. "Tell me what they know," he growled.

"OK, I will…" It was then a crazy idea came to him. It was high-risk but doing nothing was even more so. It would need split-second timing and the performance of a lifetime.

"I had a text message that told me what to do. All the details are on my phone – and you've got it. Take it out and I'll show you."

The man paused before sticking the tape back over Barney's mouth. Needing two hands to use the phone, he lowered the iron bar and fumbled in his pocket. Instead of taking out Barney's phone, he produced a small camera which flashed in Barney's face.

"Now I've got a picture to remember you by. Your last."

He looked down to examine his handiwork. It was more than Barney had hoped. As soon as the man lowered his eyes, Barney kicked up at the ceiling for all he was worth, sending the camera flying into the corner. His toe just reached its target with a crack. The strip light flew from its fitting and smashed to the floor in a spray of glowing hot fragments. In the sudden darkness, Barney tumbled over the boxes in a back-somersault and rolled across the floor, just as the iron bar smashed beside him. He scuttled away as angry shouts and thuds filled the room. The bar swung one way and then another, whooshing aimlessly into boxes and chairs. Both Barney and his attacker knew it wouldn't be long before the bar would find its target and crumple bones like paper. Barney crawled to find a corner, trying not to make a sound – or the next crunch would be his skull.

Australia Head stopped ranting and lashing in all directions when he realised that by keeping silent he'd be able to lunge at the slightest sound. In the blackness they both froze, listening, waiting, trying not to breathe. Barney could hear chewing to his right so he crept, head-down, to his left. But with hands still tied behind him, he bumped into a chair. As it scraped, the bar cracked down, smashing the wood into splinters that flew at Barney's face. The next thwack was a millimetre from his ear.

"They'll find your festering remains in one of these boxes. I'll enjoy disposing of your smashed carcass."

The bar flew in a frenzy of more thwacks, hitting the ceiling in a shower of plaster. Once more the bar crunched down, just missing Barney's shoulder. He clattered into a vacuum cleaner, rolling away just in time as it disintegrated under another strike. He shuffled past a box and felt inside. Toilet rolls. Not much good to defend himself with, but he grabbed one and threw it. He heard it hit the far wall, followed by a deafening crash from the iron bar at the other side of the room, giving him time to scramble to where he thought the door might be. His knee crunched on glass from the smashed strip-light so he stopped dead still, his heart thumping faster than in any gym display. Fear pulsed through him like never before, twisting his stomach, gripping his throat and drumming in his ears. Throwing another toilet roll, he waited for the crashing of the bar, then reached down to find a piece of glass – big enough to cut the flex binding his wrists. He felt the stickiness of blood on his fingers from the jagged edge as it chewed through the cord. Finally it gave way and released his hands. Now he could reach out in front of him and begin groping for the door. The man stood dead-still, chewing, the bar raised in his iron grip.

Barney took off his watch and peered at it under his shirt, where he could just make out the glowing digits and feel for the tiny buttons at the side. Gran's training with Braille made for sensitive fingertips, so he was able to set the alarm to go off in twenty seconds.

Laying his watch on the floor and creeping away, he sat very still in the pitch black… until a hand brushed his shoulder. He froze. The hand tensed and the iron bar swung. Suddenly a burst of mooing across the room diverted the aim. The hand pulled away and instantly the bar struck the watch before all went quiet. Sacrificing his watch had given Barney precious seconds to cower in a corner where he waited and listened. In the deathly silence he sensed the man was moving closer.

Suddenly another noise blasted near Barney's ear – his shrieking phone in the man's pocket. As long as it continued, Barney could tell exactly where the man was moving and was able to keep away from each hammer blow. He ducked and dodged the next fury of vicious swipes, his furious attacker having no idea the teenbuzz was blasting out his position. As Barney darted into the far corner from the next flurry of whacks, he peeled the tape from his mouth and stretched his hand to feel the wall. He remembered what his gran had told him about using fingers as eyes in a strange room. He tried to 'read the wall' by feeling for bumps and cracks, until his thumb touched a nail poking from the plaster. It was the nail he'd noticed just before the blackout. He could now find the light switch, which he knew was an arm's length to the right of the door. But the ringing phone was just in front of him, with the man barring his way out. It was then Barney touched a broom leaning against the wall; he grabbed it as an outrageous thought struck him. After all, he knew exactly where the enemy was and now a weapon was in his grasp. One swift crack of a broom handle over the man's head could give Barney crucial seconds to get out. He slowly lifted the broom in his sweaty palms, pausing to work out exactly where the man's head might be – hoping for a direct hit on Australia itself.

The man began speaking, scarily softly. "I'll get you with your own mobile phone. When I switch it on and shine the light, I'll see just where you are. You didn't think of that, did you? It'll be the last thing you ever see."

Barney heard the rustling breast pocket being unbuttoned. It was now or never. With all his might, he whacked the broom with such a crack that it snapped on impact. He heard the man roar and thud to the floor, crunching on broken glass. His iron bar flew into a wall and the phone clattered at Barney's feet. In an instant, he scooped it up, made a grab for the door and threw himself out into the light. He ran with no idea of where he was heading, aware only of a shadow pursuing him. The other man was on his heels. Barney darted through a doorway and found himself back in the gallery, peering down at the rest of his party in the arena far below. Before he could attract their attention, a hand grabbed his shoulder and pulled him to the floor.

Squint-Eye grunted as he slammed Barney against the gallery railings. He lifted Barney off the ground, pushing him over the rail, with a sheer drop on the other side to the arena below. Barney's phone flew out into the auditorium as he tried to cling to the rail. He was now hanging by his fingers, his feet dangling over a precipice to the stage beneath. A foot slammed onto his fingers, his grip slipped and he fell.

For a split-second Barney felt like he was flying a hang-glider again. The memory of the car rising up at him and the moment of impact on its bonnet flashed through his head. But that had been a dive from a few metres – this was serious falling. His mind swirled in a mad spin as he plunged to the stage below. His body turned and twisted as he stretched his arms. He'd won shields for his controlled mid-air manoeuvres in the gym but no contest had ever been quite like this. There were no crash mats here, but there were cables. A whole bundle of them stretched from on high, down to a lighting gantry above the stage. They were his only hope, as his flailing body plummeted.

Twisting his hips and throwing himself into a dive, Barney flew towards the cables. He grabbed with both hands, which slipped over the plastic before his desperate grip almost tugged his arms from their sockets. He held on, his legs swinging out over the stage as heads below turned to look up at a shower of sparks and a floodlight bursting like a firework. Showered with shards of splintering glass, Barney clung on and gripped the cable between his knees. He wouldn't have won a prize for style, but he'd saved himself from crashing to the arena below. Suddenly one of the straps supporting the spaghetti of cables gave way. Barney swung, Tarzan-like, down across the stage. He hit the ground running before he attempted an ungainly somersault and then bounced to a crashing halt. But there was no applause. No one appreciated a foolish show-off.

Mr Cheng was livid and didn't disguise it. "You idiot, Jones. Where the hell have you been? I've been phoning you for the last half-hour. You've missed your chance now and you're disqualified. And as for performing a ridiculous stunt like that…"

Before he'd finished shouting, the security contractor appeared at his shoulder.

"That's the kid I was telling you about. I knew he was trouble. Wrong attitude. Attention-seeker. Well, he's got the attention now – and a nice big bill for the damage…"

Barney had to tell them all. He gabbled breathlessly in a torrent of utter relief. But nobody would listen. He was a laughing stock. His ridiculous story about two men trying to kill him was far-fetched rubbish and he ought to know better. Everyone stared at him with a mixture of suspicion and total embarrassment.

"I'll prove it," he blurted in desperation. "Up in that store room. There'll be the tape he put on my mouth. I stuck it on the wall. And there'll be the flex I cut, and the broken glass. The whole place will be a wreck."

"So you trashed the stockroom? Clever lad. I'll calculate the cost of the damage."

"Aren't you going up there to look? He might still be there – I hit him hard." Barney's face lit up. "Yeah, I've just remembered. His camera. I kicked it into the corner. If you find it, there'll be all the proof you need with my picture on it! You'll need to bring a torch."

By the time they climbed all the stairs to the stockroom, Barney was feeling more confident, despite

Mr Cheng's continued lecture. As he approached the door, Barney's fear returned. What if they were in there waiting for them? Even the security man paused and raised his torch like a truncheon. He pushed the door, peered inside and his hand groped for the light switch. A strip light flickered into life and lit up the room. Boxes, chairs and cleaning equipment were stacked in neat rows, nothing out of place. No broken glass, no smashed wood, no camera lying in the corner, no signs of a shattered cow watch. There were a few dents in the ceiling, but nothing out of the ordinary – hardly the scene of recent attempted murder.

The security man turned to look at Barney with a self-satisfied smirk.

"So, what have you got to say for yourself, lad?"

Barney could only stare in utter disbelief. This couldn't be real. Speechless though he was, he could manage just about one word. He looked the man in the face and sighed. "Blimey."

CHAPTER 14

THE NATIONAL ART GALLERY, TRAFALGAR SQUARE, LONDON

Room 34 was almost empty by 8.30pm. The man who sat in a black overcoat had already studied most of the eighteenth century English paintings hanging around him on the turquoise walls. Now he continued to stare at a large canvas entitled *An Experiment on a Bird in the Air Pump*.

His stony eyes were fixed on the painted image of a scientist pumping air from a flask with a dying white cockatoo inside. Being so absorbed in the way the artist had used light on the faces in the picture, he didn't notice the woman arrive and sit beside him.

"Good evening, Brigadier. You said it was urgent."

He didn't respond for many seconds. Without taking his eyes from the painting, he said, "Exquisite brushwork. In many ways a portrayal of us all."

The woman had no idea what he meant so waited for the explanation.

"It's a masterpiece, Jan. Look at the response of each character in the drama set before us. It will be just the same after J1. Some victims will be thoughtful and reflective, some will be frightened, some will still be wrapped up in their own worlds. I guess it has always been thus. That painting is really a warning about

112

scientific ignorance. Most appropriate even today, I fear – especially given our current project."

The woman looked at her watch. "The gallery closes soon."

"It wasn't me who was late," he snapped, turning to look at her face at last, glaring disapprovingly at the eyebrow ring. "Yes, things are fairly urgent. On account of recent developments. Geoff phoned. He's convinced the boy knows too much. A natural conclusion, given the circumstances, so he's demanding that the child be dealt with."

She frowned. "I'm sure it was a coincidence that they happened to meet again. Barney turned up with his school at the Albert Hall and saw Geoff, that's all. You know how Geoff overreacts."

The brigadier sniffed and dabbed his nose with a crisp white handkerchief. "I don't want anything jeopardised because of coincidence. Nor due to a silly little schoolboy sticking his nose where it isn't wanted. At this late stage, I cannot contemplate failure."

His voice rose to a crescendo and echoed around the large room. An attendant sitting at the far end looked up, startled at such a passionate outburst.

"It's no big deal," Jan said awkwardly. "The police are hardly going to believe the boy's story. Even if they do, there's nothing to link him directly to us."

He scowled at her. "You should never have chosen the boy. It was a mistake. Admit it. You were wrong in your decision."

Before she could snap back at him, the attendant appeared at their side. "Everything all right, madam?"

She looked up angrily and tried to smile. "My friend is giving me his powerful interpretation of this painting. We're just having a slight disagreement, that's all." The attendant grunted and returned to his chair.

"I employed you, Jan, because you're a ruthless woman and as hard as nails. But I can't afford to have anyone on my team who makes errors. It was your decision to use this Barney boy but you couldn't even abduct him at the airport. I also hear you've been drinking heavily. Maybe you're not up to the pressure after all."

"I'm ten times tougher than the others," she hissed. "They don't like me so they've been telling you stuff behind my back. And I don't have a drink problem, either."

"I can smell your breath, Jan. And I'm always troubled by women who bite their nails like you. It's so unfeminine – as well as being a sign of severe anxiety. I don't tolerate mental disorder. I'm going to be watching you closely, my dear. Just like this painting."

Unable to reply, she stared ahead with fuming eyes and flushed cheeks.

After another wipe of his nose and a long pause, the brigadier stood slowly and stepped towards the painting. "The skill of the artist is to make the viewer focus on the hidden source of light, rather than notice a full moon shining in the background – as a presence of lunacy, perhaps."

She was quick to strike back. "If you're saying I'm a lunatic to choose the kid, you're wrong. You all think I'm mad, don't you? Well, I'm not, and I know what I'm doing.

My reasons are just like this artist's – to make everyone focus in a particular place. The boy was a decoy. By making MI5 focus on planes and airports, they'll miss the bigger picture."

The brigadier nodded thoughtfully. "Fair point. Nice thinking. Maybe you're not completely insane. Even so, it might still be in our interests if the child met with a fatal accident. Just to remove all possible doubt. A hit and run should do the trick. I assume you know where he lives?"

The woman stepped closer, lifting a nail-bitten hand to stroke her short spiky hair, her thumb lingering to stroke the ring in her eyebrow. "I've got his address from the luggage label I took off his bag on the plane. I really don't think it's necessary – but if you insist."

He sniffed once more and leaned forward to examine the signature on the painting. "Joseph Wright, seventeen sixty-eight. Quite wonderful. A contemporary of Jenner, of course."

His head turned with a penetrating stare from his cold piecing eyes, like a wolf's in the moonlight, she thought.

"Yes, I do insist," he added. "I suggest we refer to this little job as 'Operation Roadkill.' Just deal with it. But efficiently this time."

"Very well." She glowered. "If that's what you want. Sir." Unable to disguise the growing tension in her voice, she murmured through clenched teeth. "Leave it in my more than capable hands. Barney will be eradicated. Very soon."

CHAPTER 15

"The thing is, Laura, they all think I'm a liar, a fool, a spoilt attention-seeking brat or a raving nutcase." Barney stirred his coffee and stared through the canteen window at the rain sweeping across the school field. "And, between you and me, I'm beginning to think I'm all of those things myself."

Laura smiled and touched the back of his hand. "Oh, come on, Barney – cheer up. I'd only say you're a couple of those."

He dropped the spoon in his mug. "You what?"

"Only joking! You're really touchy lately. Don't let them upset you. I always believe what you say." She watched his eyes, but he didn't look up at her.

"It's bad enough that they all think I'm a liar. But how can I convince them about what's going on? Something scary's happening out there, Laura. And I've only glimpsed a bit of it. I reckon there's far worse to come. I mean, that Australia Head bloke I've told you about – if he knows where I live, I'm done for."

She stared at him quizzically.

"There you are." He pouted. "Now you're looking at me as though I've made it all up. I tell you, I disturbed a couple of thugs plotting something serious at the Albert Hall. I met one of them before at the airport and he was up to no good then too. I've reported him but no one seems to care. They tell me there's no proof whatsoever and it's a story I've made up 'to excuse my own reckless antics', as Mr Cheng put it. He blames an energy drink I had on the coach for making me hyperactive. I've even tried emailing the MI5 website and phoning the anti-terrorist hotline."

Laura couldn't disguise her reaction. "Careful, Barney. Don't get too carried away."

He screwed up his empty crisp packet and threw it down. "If you must know, I happen to know someone who works there – but I'm not allowed to talk about it. And no one is even bothered that I was seconds away from being murdered by a maniac with an iron bar or by a slimy, squinty-eyed psychopath who hurled me from a great height, hoping to splatter me to a pulp. And what do I get from everyone? Lectures about my lousy attitude." He stood and kicked his chair over with a clatter, before storming from the room. Heads turned at the next table as Laura was left looking at his spilled coffee trickling across the table and dribbling onto the floor. She wiped it up with a paper towel and went to find him.

Barney was sitting alone outside on the steps, seemingly unperturbed by the rain. Laura waited before going to sit beside him.

"I'm really sorry you're having a bad time lately," she said softly. "I didn't mean to upset you. It's just that I don't really understand what's been happening. Are you still having trouble with your mum's boyfriend and stuff?"

He didn't respond for the best part of a minute. Aimlessly wiping a scuff mark from his trainers, he mumbled, "I'm confused, that's all. I have been ever since that flight up to Glasgow I told you about. Everything's gone pear-shaped since then. They've all got it in for me. And now Mr Cheng won't even speak to me for letting him down. That really hurts because he was the one person who believed in me. I tried to explain but he wouldn't listen. No one listens. He told my mum, who went ballistic as she's got to pay for the damage I caused. She blamed my hormones and said it would be best if I went to live with Dad because I get on her nerves. Luckily she's going on holiday next week and my gran's coming to stay. Dad's keeping his distance since Mrs Peters emailed him about my 'deteriorating attitude'. He's gone all high and mighty, giving me lectures over the phone most nights. Everyone heard Mrs Peters announce yesterday that I'm off the ski trip because 'you simply don't deserve it, Barnaby'."

Laura smiled at his impersonation but then, returning to his self-pitying tone, he added, "I'm going to be gutted when you're off merrily skiing down the Alps while I'm stuck here or at my dad's. Can you imagine how fed up I'll be then?"

"Yeah." Laura smiled again, holding his arm. "Because I'll be here too."

"Eh?" For the first time, he looked at her directly.

She said matter-of-factly, "I told Mrs Peters I was pulling out of her ski trip because I didn't want to go without you."

"No way! There's no way you can do that. You can't. And what about your deposit?"

"Who cares? My mum made me pay it back myself but it was worth every pound, just to see Mrs Peters's face. She was well mad. I don't mind, honestly, Barney. We can go another year. It wouldn't have been much of a laugh without you. Disneyland Paris wasn't any good without you to liven it up. So I told her. Mum and Dad are fine about it. Anyway, Mrs Rickman was dead chuffed."

"Mrs Rickman? What's she got to do with it?"

"Her play. She wants me to have a singing part in *Charlie*. Rehearsals are on over Easter. And if you're interested, she says there's a part for you too."

"Get lost, Laura. No way am I prancing about on stage. I can't sing to save my life."

"I know." She giggled. "But you can do a bit of cool gymnastics to save your life. You've proved that already – particularly prancing about on the Albert Hall stage!"

"Don't remind me. But that was hardly prancing. It was life and death stuff, if only people knew it. Anyway, what's that got to do with your play?"

Laura shuffled back to shelter from a gust of cold, wet wind. "We need a stuntman. Someone to do the odd cartwheel and a bit of a tumble. You'd be great."

Barney hunched his shoulders against the stinging blast and snuggled beside her. "A stunt double, eh? Who for? Surely there's no other guy as good-looking as me!"

"It's for Greg. He's got the main part."

"Definitely not. We don't get on lately. Ever since he heard about my 'little incident' with Mr Cheng, Greg has been giving me real grief. He says I let everyone down

119

big time and spoilt the reputation of the whole school."

Laura knew how to work her charm. "Oh, go on, Barney. You look just like him from a distance. But close-up, you're much cuter! And he's useless at cartwheels and stuff."

"I've already shown myself up in front of everyone once. That's enough for me."

"But if you're in the play," she went on, giving a playful wink, "we could have great fun in Edinburgh."

"What's Edinburgh got to do with it?"

"Didn't I tell you? We're taking the show to the Edinburgh Festival in the summer. It'll be great. We'll be camping in a church hall for three weeks. Or we could all stay with your gran!"

Barney was already beaming. "Well, I might be prepared to be a stunt double. But only on one condition."

"What's that?"

"I get to do all the stunt kisses as well!" He pressed his lips firmly on her cheek.

She closed her eyes and smiled. *This could turn out quite well*, she thought.

CHAPTER 16

Gran was on top form. "Don't worry about your father, love. He's still a bit moody from when his hamster died."

"When was that?" Barney asked, aware of the mischief in her voice.

"When he was nine!" They both laughed raucously, sending Melda jumping to her feet, wagging her tail and plonking her head in Barney's lap.

"I've decided we're going to have lots of fun this week," Gran said. "It's such a long time since I've stayed in this house, it's taking me a while to re-orientate myself. I'm trying to learn exactly where everything is kept. I have to memorise a map in my head of each room. I've started with the shed. I now know the whereabouts of every single nut and bolt out there."

"Why the shed?"

"Your mother said I wasn't allowed to feed Melda in the kitchen. So the shed is Melda's dining room this week. Don't worry, I haven't touched your bike."

Barney was more interested with the presents his gran had given him. One was a bar of chocolate that he was instructed to unwrap with his eyes shut. He concentrated hard as his fingers slid over the smooth chocolate until they felt a rash of tiny bumps across its surface. His fingertips sent shapes swirling around his head and slowly formed into letters. "'With love from Gran.' I can read it! Braille chocolate!"

"There's another little something, as an early birthday present. To replace the one you smashed."

Barney could tell it was another watch as he tore off the paper. But he wasn't prepared for its alarm. It blasted a crowing cockerel when he set it off. "Gran, that is so cool! It's even louder than the cow watch. Thanks, that's brilliant."

"I'm glad you like it. Don't tell your father I gave it to you. I've also got you this, dear. It may not be to your taste, but they tell me it will get you noticed on the ski slopes."

Barney rummaged in the bag and pulled out a bright red ski hat and laughed.

"Cool! Good news and bad news. Good news – I love it. It's great. Bad news – bit of a sore point, I'm afraid. The ski trip is off."

It was after dark, halfway through a game of cards and another bar of chocolate, when Gran felt her watch. "It's late. I'll just pop out to the shed. Time to feed Melda."

"I'll do it, Gran."

"No you won't. I need to check that I know where everything is."

"But it's dark out there…" Barney stopped himself and giggled, as Gran cuffed his head. It was when she returned and they resumed their card game that Gran said something that puzzled him.

"You might have told me you'd been in the shed, dear. It took me a while to sort myself out."

"I haven't been in there for yonks," he said indignantly.

"You must have done, love. To use your bike."

"Gran, I haven't used my bike all weekend. It's your turn to lay a card—"

Gran stood up. "Come with me and I'll show you," she said forcefully. Barney managed to grab a torch from the kitchen before she led him outside and up the path to the shed.

"Now tell me, Barney. Have you not moved your bike?"

"No, that's where I always keep it."

"Take a very close look."

"Honestly, Gran, it's fine."

She stretched out her arms in front of her, letting her fingers move delicately along the top of the bench, as if playing a piano recital. One hand stopped when it came to a small hook, while her other hand groped around until it found the bike's handlebars.

"Now, young man," she began, "when I fed Melda earlier, your handlebars were directly in line with this hook. I deliberately checked. Are you accusing my dog of moving your bike a few centimetres to the left?"

Barney laughed. "Well, it's quite possible, Gran. After all, one clunk of her tail and—" Barney stopped. The beam from his torch caught a shiny glint of cut wire. "Blimey, Gran… my brake cables have been cut." He pulled on the brakes and watched in horror as the wheels still turned.

"Why ever would anyone do that? It seems like vandalism," she said sharply. Barney had a different reaction. He said nothing, as the colour drained from his face. The sabotage in front of him only confirmed his greatest fear. They were definitely after him… and they were here.

CHAPTER 17

Hidden eyes were watching. They stared from a white transit van with blackened windows and false number plates. It was parked down Barney's road, with a zoom lens focused through its windscreen onto his side gate. As Barney emerged from his front door in his new red ski hat and black school bag slung over his shoulder, the camera zoomed in and clicked. Face recognition software in a laptop connected to the camera immediately analysed the photograph. In seconds, it processed the data from key points and angles on Barney's image, to produce his unique face-print. Within a few more seconds it was matched with a digital image taken of him at the airport, and produced the result: AFFIRMATIVE. This was definitely the intended target.

The van driver swore when he realised Barney was walking on the path and not riding his bike. It would have been far easier to strike at the bottom of the hill where the sabotaged brakes were supposed to make Barney gain speed and lose control. Now it was time for Plan B. Operation Roadkill would have to become Operation Pathkill. The engine revved and its masked driver slammed it into gear, ready to accelerate in an instant and career over the pavement.

Barney continued walking, absorbed in his iPod music and oblivious to the throaty rumbles and jets of exhaust fumes just a few metres ahead. He was already late for school so he quickened his pace before darting across the road. The van driver swore again at the missed opportunity. He let Barney walk past and down the hill, before he released the clutch and the van lurched forward. It quickly gained speed, churning out even blacker smoke as it clattered over the kerb, ready to mow down the target and crush him against a wall.

Barney didn't see the shadow speeding towards him. He was totally unaware of the bumper about to smash into his legs and the front wheel racing to crush his body into a lifeless mess. He had no idea the bonnet was about to slam into him as he darted to his left up Baker Alley between two high wooden fences. Right behind him, the front bumper buckled on impact with a wall as the van scraped across bricks with an ear-splitting screech. Grit, mud, sparks and chunks of brick flew in all directions. The battered vehicle bounced back onto the road with a roar from the engine, a crunch of the suspension and a crack of the exhaust pipe clunking the kerb.

With hands pushed firmly in his pockets, Barney was still blissfully unaware of the scene behind him as he whistled his way along the alley, across the main road and on through the school gates – a full minute before the white van squealed to a halt outside, with its driver still swearing. It would now have to be Plan C. That meant waiting until the end of school to strike, when Barney would cross the main road again… for the last time. Operation Roadkill would now have to risk other casualties and more witnesses. The driver cursed and thumped the dashboard.

The wait was even longer than expected as it was well after five o'clock when Barney and Laura finally appeared at the school gates. The lone occupant of the battered white van parked opposite watched impatiently. The zoom lens was poised.

"So what do you reckon?" Laura asked. "I thought it was a good rehearsal."

"Yeah," Barney said, rummaging around in his bag. "You were great. I loved it."

"So you're definitely up for being stuntman?"

"Sure. Hey, what do you think of my gran's present?" He plonked the bright red ski hat on his head as Laura squealed with delight.

"That's so cool! I want one!"

A voice behind them growled, "Who'd have a double like him?"

"Hi, Greg. I thought your song went well just now." Barney grinned beneath his hat.

"Oh yeah?" Greg sneered, pushing past them. "A shame we've got a failure on board who lets down the gym team. An unreliable little loser in a naff tea cosy". He crossed the road towards the corner shop without looking back.

"I told you he doesn't like me," Barney said.

"We'll work on him. Anyway, I do!" Laura pulled his arm and they, too, headed to the kerb to cross the road.

The van moved out of the lay-by before slamming its brakes and reversing back into position. Again the driver swore. He could so easily have hit them but his instructions had been clear. A clean kill and no other

126

casualties. He could only sit and wait while his target went into the shop.

"How about some chocolate raisins?" Barney took two packets from the shelf. "I'd better get some for Gran, too."

Greg finished paying for some torch batteries. "Don't eat those sweets all at once. I don't want an obese stunt double!"

Barney responded with a sarcastic smile and a stronger gesture. Greg glared back as his hand shot out and snatched Barney's hat. He laughed mockingly as he ran from the shop. "I bet stunt double can't run double fast!"

Pulling the hat down over his ears, Greg darted off down the street, with his black bag slung over his shoulder. He turned back to wave and jeer. Immediately the van revved and shot forward. There wasn't time for Greg to shout to Laura at the shop door before the vehicle mounted the pavement and slammed into him. He didn't stand a chance, as he crumpled under its thundering wheels and the axle crushed his skull. Greg's buckled body lay sprawled across the path, his head face-down in the road beside the red ski hat and a trickle of blood in the gutter. He didn't move. Nothing moved.

Apart from the squeal of tyres racing away up the street, everything fell deathly still and eerily silent, like an old photograph drained of colour – frozen in time. The only sound came from Laura whimpering at the shop door.

"Oh my God!"

Barney held her, open-mouthed, before running to the roadside and screaming, "Greg! Greg!"

A single battery rolled along the path, spun into the gutter and clattered down a drain. The other was still in Greg's hand, bent between snapped fingers.

The van roared through the housing estate, rattling round bends and skidding over junctions. It sped down a track and along a service road to an industrial estate. In a cloud of dust, it slammed to a halt behind a row of derelict sheds. The driver jumped out, removed his mask and, with bag over his shoulder, walked purposefully towards a tunnel through the railway embankment. Halfway along in the darkness, he removed his boiler suit and emerged the other end dressed in an immaculate jacket, white shirt and tie. He cast the overalls into a wheelie bin and continued his way towards the railway station. Within minutes he was sitting on a train, his laptop open on a table in the first class carriage. Once the train began moving, he slipped his hand into his case and pressed the remote control handset. From the train window he saw the van erupt in a somersault of flames. Fire ripped through its shattered windscreen as smoke rolled up into the sky. He smiled as he turned away to look at the screen of his laptop, while adjusting his earpiece. He could hear radio messages from the emergency services clearly. Three terms in particular. Juvenile. Fatality. Dead at the scene.

Once more the man in the train smirked as he watched the countryside flash past outside. He tapped the keyboard in front of him and a line of letters stretched across the screen: 'Operation Roadkill. Mission Accomplished'. He smugly clicked on 'send'.

Outside the corner shop, long after the ambulance, police cars and crowds had gone, a single bouquet lay on the kerb. A small card fluttered in the wind, with just five words written in a very unsteady hand:

Greg, I'm so sorry. Barney.

Just behind, six words stood out on a news stand: 'SCHOOLBOY KILLED IN HIT AND RUN'. Before long it was surrounded by football scarves, soft toys and school ties. The flowers piled into a mound, with many cards expressing only one word: *why*?

Not far away a burnt-out van smouldered long into the night, its smoky wisps drifting over stunned and unusually deserted streets.

CHAPTER 18

THE ROYAL COLLEGE OF SURGEONS MUSEUM, EDINBURGH

The Surgeon's Hall was empty apart from the rows of glass cases containing skeletons, skulls and pickled organs. A figure stood at the entrance, unbuttoning a tailored charcoal coat and peering down his nose at the statue of a corpse. He stepped into the room and checked his watch against a clock on the wall.

"No doubt you'll tell me I'm late." A familiar oily voice came from behind him.

"I've known worse." The brigadier slowly removed his leather gloves while scrutinising the death mask of a famous murderer from 1829. "How deliciously gruesome." He turned to face the man behind him. "I have a couple of keys for you, Geoff. The apartment is yours for five months until the end of August. Very tasteful and far from cheap." He handed him the keys with smug satisfaction. "How ironic that I should be handing keys to my ex-gaoler who spent every day rattling keys beneath my nose. That was until I persuaded you and Jan to embark on more worthwhile careers. What fortune that, of all the prison staff, I found two with such malice and greed. Just make sure you keep the apartment locked at all times."

"Of course – old habits die hard. I know the address," Geoff said, chewing vigorously.

"Good. You're costing me a fortune one way and another." The brigadier managed half a smile. "But you're worth it."

"Operation Roadkill was worth it, too. It was money well spent to get that kid out the way. I hated the little brat. Good riddance, if you ask me. My shoulder's still dodgy after our punch-up at the Albert Hall."

"You're in the right place to get it looked at." More of a smile. "Yes, it seems Jan acted properly this time and hired a hitman to do a good job. Swift and efficient, the way I like things. And no more worries of an irritating Barney jamming a spanner in the works. I trust you checked the hitman got the right target."

"I can't say I have. But I'm sure Jan wouldn't get that wrong. I know she's hitting the bottle lately but I reckon she seems reliable."

The brigadier pondered as he squinted into a glass cabinet containing what looked like a leather-bound notebook. "Things aren't always what they seem." He sniffed. "This, for example, is not leather but human skin – peeled from the carcass of a murderer." He stood upright and said abruptly, "I want you to check on everything Jan does. She is showing signs of strain and I can no longer trust her. You know what happens to those I can't trust, Geoff?"

Geoff nodded and chewed even faster, as the brigadier continued in an amused whisper. "At least I know I can rely on you. You might be an ignorant brute but you get things done to my satisfaction. You'd kill your own grandmother if I asked you."

"How do you know I haven't done it already?" He wheezed and threw his head back, grinning evilly

"You're totally heartless, Geoff. That's why I pay you so well."

"Glad to hear it, Brigadier. So how's your side of things going?"

The brigadier puffed out his chest with obvious pride. "Like clockwork. And some of us value clockwork more than others. Phipps Pharmaceuticals is even ahead of schedule, I am delighted to say. I'm currently stocking a couple of high security warehouses on the other side of the city with the surplus. I'll need you to keep a regular check on things over there as well as head up the site for J1. We've upped production of TATP and scent-screen. Needless to say, it's vital the whole project stays firmly under wraps with the utmost secrecy. The fewer involved, the better. From now on, always use coded messaging and encrypted systems." He lowered his voice to a whisper again. "Should you suspect anyone, particularly Jan, of anything improper, dispose of them. Clear?"

"Perfectly, Brigadier."

"Good. Now for a little quiz." He polished his glasses with a silk handkerchief. "Take a look in that cabinet over there. For a clue as to why I gave my company its name."

Geoff did as he was told and obediently peered into the display. His blotchy skin glistened under the spotlights and his Australia birthmark shone in a film of sweat. "Oh no, not Jenner again." He smirked with a smarmy politeness that belied his boredom.

"Exactly. And the boy's name?"

Geoff strained to read the small print, chewing frantically, sweating freely. "Oh, I see. James Phipps. You named your company after a kid?"

"Indeed. He was Jenner's eight-year-old medical guinea pig in seventeen ninety-six and the results eventually changed the world. I intend to do just the same. But whereas his success took nearly two hundred years, we will be working on a shorter time-scale. For, as I keep telling you, time matters."

"It will in five months. When the fireworks really start!" Geoff's sickly snigger drifted around the displays marked 'History of Surgery', seeming to linger at the hanged murderer's skeleton – a notorious uncouth brute.

The similarity to the brutal thug chewing noisily beside him wasn't lost on the brigadier. His grey wolf eyes narrowed menacingly above a more-than-satisfied smile.

CHAPTER 19

The nightmare Barney had witnessed was sometimes too much to bear. He was certain it should have been him inside that coffin covered in flowers in the hearse driving past the school gates to the funeral. He struggled to focus on the floral display in football colours spelling a single word: GREG.

When police officers spoke to the whole school in a special assembly in the sports hall, they asked for anyone with any information about Greg's death to talk to them in confidence in the library. A woman police officer sat writing in the librarian's office when Barney entered the room. He recognised her as the one who had taken his statement on the night of Greg's death.

"Hello, Barney," she said. "I wondered if you'd come for a chat. We thought you might want to amend your statement after you've calmed down a little and had chance to think things through. You've had a horrible time, so how are you now?"

"Much the same." He sat expressionless in the chair in front of her. "I don't need to change my statement, I just want to make sure you understand everything."

The officer sat back in her swivel chair, twisting one way then the other. "Go ahead, Barney. I'm listening."

He took a deep breath and began at full speed. "I'm more convinced than ever that Korova killed Greg. He was mown down because of me as he was wearing my red hat and they mistook him for me—"

The woman raised her hand. "Woah, woah, hold on a minute. You said all this before when you were obviously suffering from deep shock. Are you still telling me you believe you're the intended victim of terrorists?"

"Exactly. And you need to tell MI5. Aries needs to know."

"So you're sticking with this MI5 story of a boy of thirteen being trained as a special agent at a big house in the country where he crashed a hang-glider? So how do you suggest I check out your story? How can I contact this Aries, I wonder?"

"I don't know. I've tried but I can't get anywhere."

"Nor can we. The security services have no record of you, Barney."

"That's because they took me off their database."

She sat back, with eyebrows raised, then flicked through her notes. "So where was this big house exactly?"

"I've no idea. About a couple of hours from here and by a river. If you could contact Seb, he would help."

"Seb who?"

"I don't know."

"Is there anyone else, with a full name, who could verify your story?"

"You could always try Tarquin. He's the son of the Home Secretary who I had—"

She put down her pen and looked up sternly. "That's enough, Barney. You only know him from the news and it's not funny. I have to say, at thirteen you're a little old to have an imaginary friend called Seb."

"I've told you, it's all true! So was the attack on me at the Albert Hall that no one will believe."

"Ah yes, that little business," she said patronisingly. "I've just had a chat with both Mr Cheng and Mrs Peters, who say they know you well. They seem to think you may be prone to the occasional flight of fancy."

He kicked at the desk. "That's rubbish. No one ever listens to me."

She sighed and forced another insincere smile. "Barney, I'm not blaming you for trying to make sense of all this in whatever way helps you. Dealing with sudden death for the first time, especially at your age, can be a traumatic experience. But you do need to understand and come to terms with what is real and what is not. Is your mother still away and your father in Scotland?"

"They don't know about all this. I had to sign the Official Secrets Act."

"Did you, indeed? So what can you talk about to your mother?"

"Not much at the moment. Since she came back from holiday she's been too busy. Anyway, she's thinking about getting married again, so we only argue."

She nodded and gave a knowing glance. "Barney, I deal with a lot of young people who often feel neglected and deserted at times of distress, and it's quite normal to want to be noticed and to crave some attention. We can offer you some counselling if you—"

Barney stood up angrily. "So you still don't believe a word I'm telling you?"

"Sometimes we all have different ideas of what is real or what is the absolute truth."

Barney threw up his arms with a grunt of despair and headed for the door. "So what part of TERRORIST ATTACK don't you understand?" He slammed the door behind him and stormed down the corridor – before the tears finally flowed.

For days and sleepless nights Barney felt numb and bewildered. On his birthday, which he dismissed as the worst ever, he sat subdued, wrestling with emotions he never knew he had. He couldn't talk to Laura, who was also struggling with her own shock and grief. She seemed unusually distant and cold, as if she, too, blamed him for Greg's death. When he tried to talk to Mr Cheng about his fears of a hitman after him, he got a stony response.

"Let's not go there, Barney. Don't make a drama out of Greg's tragedy. Maybe you should read the story of *The Boy Who Cried Wolf* and realise the problem with tall stories. One day your life might depend on people needing to trust your word."

Despite everything, the show went on. Rehearsals continued with renewed purpose, with the same sentiment expressed by everyone: "We're doing this for Greg". Barney was determined to do something positive and try to make sense of the tragedy, as well as all those nagging fears and guilt swirling in his head.

Mrs Peters didn't help matters. "You've been much quieter lately, Barney. Let's hope this means you're turning a corner and your attitude is on the up. Perhaps your involvement in the school production is just what the doctor ordered."

This time he chose not to answer back. Instead, he headed to the hall for the technical rehearsal of the show. During the finale he had to jump from a springboard and flip across the stage in a spectacular series of cartwheels, before tumbling over a balcony (supposedly into the sea) and soaking the front rows. He lay sprawled, panting on a crash mat, just as the stage manager threw out a bucketful of water.

After the final chorus and curtain call, Mrs Rickman screamed with delight and all the cast cheered. Barney couldn't help feeling his reputation might at last be on the rise. Then came the news that their show would run at the Demarco Roxy Art House in Edinburgh for three weeks. August couldn't come soon enough.

Walking home from the rehearsal, Barney crossed the street to the corner shop and stood momentarily at the spot where Greg had been killed. "It should have been me down there, Greg. It was my fault. I so wish there's some way I could bring you back."

Being so absorbed in his thoughts, it took him a while to make sense of the letters scrawled across the news stand behind him. The headline was bold and chilling. 'HOME SECRETARY'S SON FOUND DEAD'. Barney rushed into the shop to buy a paper. He read with astonishment that Tarquin had been found drowned in the River Thames after taking an overdose. It was suggested he must have taken his own life. Members of the government were rallying round to support the Home Secretary.

Barney sat for hours on his bed with his head in his hands. Until recently he hadn't known anyone his own age who had died. Now there were two. He hadn't liked either of them and they certainly hadn't liked him. Their deaths were still tragic and he couldn't help wishing he'd been a bit kinder to them both. Regrets and big questions spun around his head all night. Even thoughts of the first performance of the show the following evening failed to intrude on his inner turmoil. He'd never felt so alone.

"I came to see the show last night, Barney." Mrs Peters was speaking to him genially for once. "You're a bit of a star. It was good to see your father in the audience. He said he was very proud of you."

"Really?" Barney was genuinely surprised. "He didn't say much to me other than he'll bring my gran to the show when we're in Edinburgh in the summer."

"I'm sure she'll be most impressed, Barney."

He slumped over a desk.

"Are you all right?" Mrs Peters asked.

"Just heart failure, miss. I've never heard you use those two words together before."

She stared at him, puzzled.

"'Impressed' and 'Barney'. There wasn't an 'attitude' anywhere in the sentence."

Her glare said it all. "Don't overstep the mark, young man. We wouldn't want to fall out before Edinburgh, would we?"

Barney suddenly looked worried. "Miss?"

"Didn't Mrs Rickman tell you? I'll be one of the members of staff coming to keep my eye on you all in

August. I shall be there to make sure you in particular behave."

She smiled and flounced from the room, fully aware of the impact. Barney was still staring at the door long after she'd gone. "You've got to be joking!"

When he told Laura about who their minder would be in Edinburgh, Barney looked particularly gloomy.

"Don't worry, Barney. We'll still have fun. And just remember that we'll be raising money for Greg's memorial fund."

A book slammed to the floor with a crash.

"What did you do that for?" Laura was startled.

"I'm so angry. I know I wasn't the best of mates with Greg but I reckon he deserves better than a miserable memorial fund. What good is that? The least he deserves is for his killer to get caught. The times I've told the police who I think did it. The times I've tried to email, phone and text our so-called security service. If only I could get hold of Seb, he'd know what to do. No one will listen to me. But I'm determined to find whoever did this and make sure they pay for what they've done – and I don't mean to some daggy memorial fund to buy a pathetic park bench with a rusty plaque." His voice cracked, his face flushed and his eyes filled. But he hadn't finished yet. "I know big boys aren't supposed to cry. Maybe it's all this theatrical stuff getting me dramatic and hyper-emotional. Maybe I'm just tired and irritable, but it's really got to me lately. Tarquin may have been a stuck-up twit but he didn't deserve to lose it all. I know you haven't got a clue what I'm talking about, but he and I had a fight and I feel terrible about it now. Laura, I've had enough and I'm just so damn sick of it all."

He stomped off, leaving Laura even more bewildered and considerably upset herself.

Mrs Peters was unbearable at the end-of-show party.

"I thought you were all wonderful. There wasn't a dry eye in the house. As Publicity Officer, I'm so delighted we were a sell-out. Smile, Barney!" She flashed her camera and took another slurp of punch. "A fabulous picture! I'll put that one on the website."

Barney reacted instantly. "No! Please don't."

"What's the matter, Barney? Frightened of too much fan mail?" She giggled loudly.

"I just don't want my picture or name out there, thank you, miss."

"Too late, my dear. I've already put on a picture of you in a mid-air crash dive." She looked very pleased with herself but Barney felt the anger rising inside him.

"Not with my name, I hope."

"But of course. We don't want to hide your light under a bushel, do we?" She giggled again, taking more swigs of the clearly potent punch.

Barney wasn't going to give up. "But you need parents' permission to put things like that on the internet."

Her smile vanished. "Barney, do you really think I don't know the correct procedures? Of course I've got permission. Your father said it was perfectly in order and above board."

"Well, nobody asked me!" He hadn't meant to shout and everyone turned to look at where the outburst had come from.

Mrs Peters was speechless before her tone changed to that of 'She Who Must Be Obeyed'.

"Barnaby, there is no need to shout or to get on your high horse. I know you're now a member of the cast, but there's no need to become a spoilt prima donna."

"Miss, it's important that my name and details aren't out there for all to see. I'm not being all dramatic about this. It's just that I have my reasons… and my rights."

"Rights?" Now it was her turn to raise her voice. "Don't be ridiculous. You're making a mountain out of a molehill and you know it. It's simply a picture of the back of your head with a caption, that's all. It's nothing for you to start getting stroppy about, young man."

"I'm trying not to be stroppy, miss. But what if someone Googles my name? Up I'll pop."

"So what's the big deal? Are you concerned the FBI might track you down at last?" Once more she looked delighted with her own sarcasm.

"I want my details taken off." Even Barney was surprised at how forceful he sounded. But his determination was driven by fear. Fear of 'them'. Fear of a white van returning.

It was time for Mrs Peters to play the concerned and disappointed tutor.

"Just when I thought you were turning a corner, you suddenly let me down again, Barnaby. Your attitude repeatedly gets in the way and once more you fail to understand. For such a bright boy you can sometimes be so incredibly stupid."

Barney knew what he wanted to say was wrong. He was fully aware that he would pay the price. But, right then, he could take no more of this ghastly woman to whom he referred as 'The Control Freak'.

"Yeah, whatever…" He walked away muttering, rather than blurting out what he really wanted to say. Even so, he knew his sins would soon come back to haunt him.

Mrs Peters sparked off the next spat just a few weeks later.

"Barnaby, you'll be delighted to learn that, despite my better judgment, I have removed all reference to you on the website. However, it doesn't seem to have reduced the number of your stalkers beating a path to my door." She smiled with absolute relish, knowing that Barney had no idea what she was talking about and that he was sure to be in her power by begging to know more. She was wrong.

"Really?" he said half-heartedly. He didn't feel like playing another of her games, particularly as Gran had been unwell since his birthday and he was worried about her.

"Well, aren't you going to ask me who she was?" Her self-satisfied smirk refused to budge.

"Who?" Barney looked out of the classroom window at the blazing June sunshine.

"The journalist who came to interview me. But she seemed particularly interested in you, as it happens."

"In what way?"

Mrs Peters was clearly irritated by Barney's lack of excitement. "Is this heat getting to you? Or maybe it's stardom! She came down from Scotland to do a piece on our show. She was particularly interested in what effect poor Greg has had on us all but then she mentioned you. 'What about the lovely Barney Jones?', she asked. She wanted to know how you were coping with being in the limelight with your trampoline skills."

Barney wondered at first if this was another of Mrs Peters's attempts to be funny.

"Sure, miss. Nice try at winding me up. But you forgot an important bit of detail. I don't use a trampoline in the show so how would she know I do trampolining?"

"She happened to know that you'd won the odd trophy for bouncing around."

Barney felt a shiver run through him. He stared at Mrs Peters in absolute horror.

"This woman," he said quickly, "did she have an eyebrow ring by any chance? With a snake's pink eye?"

Mrs Peters frowned. "No, Barney. Nothing of the sort. No jewellery that I recall – other than a rather smart watch."

Barney's stomach churned. "Not Elaine, surely. Big blonde hair and loads of make-up?"

"I hope you're not going to get all sulky and dramatic again, young man," she bristled. "In actual fact, you're quite wrong about her appearance. More auburn, if you ask me."

He reached out and almost touched her. "What about the watch? Describe the watch."

"Keep calm, Barney. I can't think why all this matters. It's just that I happened to comment on her watch, that's all. A sort of black and silver bracelet that lit up rather tastefully. Quite pricy, I would imagine."

"Seiko?"

"I believe so. Listen, why is all this so important to you?"

"How about a plaster on the back of her hand?" He was becoming increasingly agitated.

"Not that I noticed." She paused thoughtfully. "Maybe a little scar, now you mention it."

Barney turned away and looked through the window for a long time. "What did this woman want, exactly?"

"I told you. She's a journalist on one of the Scottish newspapers. She had quite a strong Edinburgh accent and even used a little tartan notebook for scribbling down my comments. They're running a feature on our show and I happily told her everything. All good publicity. She only mentioned Greg and you in passing."

"What about us? What did she ask?"

She hesitated and looked uncomfortable. "Just a misunderstanding. The woman had the impression it was you who'd… had the tragic accident."

Her words triggered an outburst that set Barney off like a firework. "Accident? Accident? That was no accident! And now you've gone blabbing all sorts to her. That woman, Mrs Peters, wasn't a journalist. She just so happens to be involved in a terrorist plot and wants me in a coffin. It shouldn't have been Greg under the wheels of that van but me. That's why I didn't want anything about me going on the internet. That's why,

Mrs Peters, it would have been rather nice if you'd managed to keep your mouth shut for a change."

They stared at each other in stunned silence for a full five seconds before he stormed from the room as tears spilled down his cheeks. All he could hear behind him was a torrent of disconnected words. "Outrageous... ridiculous... absurd." No doubt there was an 'attitude' or two thrown in as well.

The last Barney heard as he stomped outside into the blazing sunshine was Mrs Peters almost screaming at him from her window. "Just wait till I phone your father."

Chapter 20

"I hope you like Mozart, another genius of the eighteenth century. I guess you must, as you're here in such good time for the concert." Dressed in dinner jacket and bow tie, the brigadier looked every part the suave man of taste that he liked to portray.

"How could I possibly be late with the special watch you gave me to keep me forever punctual?" His companion glanced at her elegant black and silver bracelet-watch. In her claret sequinned evening dress, she looked nothing like any of the characters she played in her usual course of work. Now her hair was short and dark, and her striking face had only the most subtle make-up.

The brigadier poured her a glass of champagne and passed a menu. "We have an hour until the concert. But you know how important time is to me. As I always say, 'Better late than never, but never late is better'."

She raised her glass. "To next month… and excellent timing."

He echoed her words and chinked his glass against hers. "So tell me your findings. As actress and assessment officer, tell me your appraisal of the risk."

147

She lowered her glass and took a long breath. "So far, so good. We got rid of the young MI5 lad before he could pass anything on. We had no idea he was the son of the Home Secretary but we did a good job in making it look like suicide. So we nipped that particular threat in the bud."

"Excellent." He waved to attract a waiter's attention. After ordering the most expensive bottle on the wine list, he leaned forward and whispered, with an edge of concern, "What of that Barney boy? I paid good money to have him removed by a hitman. I now understand Jan got that wrong, too. What have you found out since I promoted you to be my personal assistant, Philippa?"

"I carried out a few routine Google searches to check out his funeral but I discovered he's alive and well, and performing in a play. So I went hotfoot to investigate. It appears your hitman got the wrong boy. But, I have to say, I fail to see how Barney is a threat to us. He's hardly likely to jeopardise anything, is he?"

"It was Geoff's idea to get rid of the boy after an encounter at the Albert Hall and I was inclined to agree. So what is your assessment? On a threat scale of one to ten, where does this Barney fall?"

She thought for a few seconds as she swirled the wine in her glass. "In my view, zero. Let's face it, that boy is hardly in the top league. He knows nothing. Although it was Jan's decision to choose him, it was me who first spotted him at the airport in my 'blind woman guise' and I have to admit I have a certain affection for the lad. And I so loved being Elaine, his dumb air hostess. One of my better characters, I feel."

"You are the mistress of disguise and a talent to behold." He leaned forward and spoke softly. "Your father would be most proud, I'm sure. He was the only officer in my regiment with good taste and impeccable judgement. I'm delighted you take after him, my dear."

"I still miss him. My hatred of your regiment for what they did to him doesn't fade with the years, either. They still call it friendly fire but to me it will always be murder. That's why I'm delighted to be involved with your revenge against them."

"You're more than just involved," he said. "You're my second in command for the whole operation. I value your judgement, Philippa. However, I'm not sure if I agree that the Barney boy can be totally forgotten."

She shrugged and added casually, "The fact that he'll be up here performing at the Festival Fringe during J1 is of no consequence. I'm sure he's harmless."

The brigadier raised an eyebrow. "He's coming up here? On my patch?" He sniffed and fiddled with his cufflinks. "In that case, I shall have to prepare something."

"I'm happy to monitor the situation," she said. "Discreetly, of course."

"Something else to jot in that tartan notebook of yours." He stroked the silver salt cellar with his finger before adding, with a cold stare that couldn't disguise the cruelty in his eyes, "Despite your reassuring assessment, I still want that boy eliminated. Just to be on the safe side. I must also decide what to do about Jan. She's making errors and becoming unstable. When I informed her that she must now take orders from you, she appeared quite neurotic. Whereas you, my dear…"

149

He held her fingers and kissed a small scar on the back of her hand. "You're so sophisticated and civilised, while the others in our team are coarse and vulgar. You and Jan are each like your hairstyles. You're elegant, stylish and in complete control, while she's severe, spiky and fiery!"

Philippa laughed as she lifted her glass to sip some wine. "Jan's certainly brash and blunt. She's never hidden the fact that she dislikes me. Now I'm her boss, she's likely to be even more bolshie – or drink herself to distraction. I'm afraid I don't like her either, but I have to say I do quite like the Barney lad. There's something sparky yet charmingly cheeky about him."

The brigadier unrolled his napkin, arranged it carefully over his lap and smirked. "So it appears, my dear Philippa, that I have competition for your affections. All the more reason for a pre-emptive strike. It seems that boy may well get far more than he bargained for from his little trip north of the border. This time I think a good old-fashioned Scottish murder is called for. With style… and razor-sharp precision."

Chapter 21

Immediately the coach pulled up outside the Demarco Roxy Art House, all on board cheered excitedly, apart from Mrs Peters. She wasn't impressed by whoops and whistles. Mrs Rickman laughed and addressed the party through a microphone.

"This is it, everyone. Our home for the next three weeks. What you've all worked so hard for, you splendid bunch!" More cheers.

Mrs Peters took the microphone. "Right, now, listen to me. I have some important things to say and it is *essential* you all pay the utmost attention." A few stifled groans came from the back seat.

"Most of you are old enough and sensible enough to know what we expect of you. However, some of the younger ones…" She paused and looked directly at Barney, who smiled back angelically, much to her annoyance. "Yes, some of you need to be reminded not only of standards of behaviour required at all times, but also of potential risks in an unfamiliar busy city. Firstly, at no time is anyone to go off on their own. I need to know where everyone is at all times. You will be allowed to explore in pairs or groups only when you've checked with me first. Everyone has a list of rules and times and when to check in with me. I take a register every night before bed at ten o'clock." She ignored the reaction from the back. "You all have my mobile number and I have yours so it is *essential* we all keep these switched on whenever we are out and about. I hope I make myself clear, Barney."

"Perfectly, Mrs Peters. Just chillax!" She bristled at the giggles that erupted around him.

"Needless to say," she went on much louder, "you should not leave valuables in your bags, nor invite anyone you happen to meet back to the dormitories. In fact, not so much dorms as camp beds in a church hall somewhere nearby. Right, we'll synchronise watches, get ourselves settled and meet on stage for a full rehearsal in an hour. Any questions?"

Barney's hand shot up. "Yes, miss. Can I ask you to tuck me in each night and read me a bedtime story?" Squeals and cheers. Even Mrs Rickman laughed. Everyone knew he was dicing with danger. After a tense pause, Mrs Peters smiled unconvincingly.

"How about a horror story?"

"Just the job, miss."

"Good. I'll read you your next school report." The response was as she'd wished but the point had to be made publicly. "Barney, once we've all got sorted, I think you and I will have a little chat. Just to remind you who's boss. Only then will I 'chillax'." Sniggers. It was clear to all that he'd have to pay dearly for his little joke.

"I shall be keeping a close eye on you, Barney, throughout our time here." The lecture began a few minutes later. "We've had our ups and downs in the past but I'm prepared to call a truce if you understand what I expect of you. My rules are simple. No nonsense. Let's forget all those fantasy ideas about bogeymen being after you or agents hiding round every corner. This is the real world, with real people. Crowds of them. They don't want to be embarrassed by a schoolboy with an overly vivid imagination. Our time here can be a big turning point for you and I want you to make this a great learning opportunity. I'm sure you can do it and won't let me down. I'm sure I don't have to warn you of the consequences. For instance, I can easily call your father and he'll come and collect you instantly. After all, you're fourteen now, so let's see a new, mature Barney."

"Yes, miss." Barney gave the sad spaniel look, not that it ever worked on Mrs Peters. He knew for certain it wasn't worth arguing – which was the only thing he *was* certain about lately.

"I'm going to turn over a new leaf, miss. Even you will be dead proud of me."

They each smiled even though they both knew he hadn't sounded entirely genuine.

After a full rehearsal and sorting camp beds in the church hall, it was sight-seeing time. Laura was keen to explore.

"Miss says you and I can go together, Barney. She says I'm a good influence on you. Let's tackle the big city! How about a stroll to the castle?"

"Any idea where it is?" Barney was already searching for his sat nav. "Gran's leant me her vibrating-rings GPS for finding our way around all the alleys and side streets."

Laura laughed. "The castle's big enough to find without that. We saw it from the coach. It's on top of a dirty great rock!"

"Just give me the postcode and I'll lead you there."

She found the castle website on her phone and Barney tapped in the postcode, then slid on the rings. "Come on then, it's twitching already. To the castle, Macduff!"

They strode through the packed streets, with Barney calling 'right' or 'left' each time the rings on his fingers tingled. The castle grew in front of them, through the vast crowds already gathering for an evening show of military bands and fireworks. The infectious excitement buzzed through every street, as Laura read aloud from a guidebook above the noise of the heaving multitudes and rowdy street performers.

"The Edinburgh Festival Fringe is the largest arts festival in the world, with theatre, comedy, dance, music and musicals, children's and street theatre, magic and mime. This festival transforms the streets of Edinburgh throughout August, with buskers, street theatre and live entertainment filling nearly every cobblestone. Over two thousand shows and eighteen thousand performers entertain more than one and a half million people in two hundred and fifty venues across the city."

Barney shouted over the hubbub, "That's us! They've all come to see our show!"

Jostling through the hoards of people were actors dressed in costumes, handing out leaflets for shows.

"We'll be doing that tomorrow," Laura shrieked. "I can't wait!"

The first matinee performance came to a spectacular finale, with Barney's timing being perfect, despite a few technical problems with a noisy smoke machine and a faulty follow-spot. The straggle of an audience clapped heartily, then it was time for aggressive marketing. Barney and Laura's patch for inviting crowds to the next show was part of the Royal Mile. They thrust flyers into hands and enthused to anyone who would listen, just as a voice called from a sea of faces. "Barney!"

A hand was suddenly patting his shoulder enthusiastically. "Whatever are you doing here?" Barney was amazed to be shaking hands with Seb.

"Hi Seb! I'm dishing out flyers for our show."

"Flyers!" Seb roared. "The last I saw of you was definitely as a non-flyer! But I won't mention your hang-glider skills. It's great to see you. I've wanted to get in touch for ages but…" He saw Laura and stopped himself.

"It's OK," Barney said. "Laura's safe. Seb, I've so been dying to tell you loads of stuff. It's just that—"

"Not now, Barney. I'll see you soon." He pulled away and was jostled into a torrent of people.

"So what are you doing here?" Barney called after him, reaching out to push a flyer into his hand.

"I start uni here next month. Look, must go. I'll be in touch. Soon. Honest." He was whisked away by the current, disappeared into the swirling crowd and was gone.

"Who's that?" Laura asked. "He looks cool."

"Then it will be my pleasure to introduce you to Seb properly sometime."

Seb appeared out of the blue at the end of a show. The cast had just finished their curtain call to an enthusiastic audience when a loud American in a baseball cap and dark glasses barged back stage. "Hey, you guys, that was real swell. And you, junior, I just loved your wonderful gymnastic routine at the end there." He shook Barney's hand enthusiastically, pushing a note into his palm with a wink. "Mind how you go now!" He waved and was gone.

Laura whispered in Barney's ear, "Wasn't that Seb?"

"Shush." He crept away to read the note in private.

Meet me tonight. Alone. Urgent. 12.30am at Pleasance Courtyard. Under tree. Destroy this quick.

Barney said nothing. He'd have to creep out when everyone was in bed and ignore the risks. He tore up the note into tiny pieces and threw them like confetti into the warm breeze.

After nights of shows and parties, everyone was shattered. Audiences were growing all the time and the first official review gave the show a five star rating. All performers were ready for bed well before lights-out. By midnight, all was quiet and dark in the boys' sleeping quarters, although the glow of streetlights spilled in through high windows at either end of the hall. Barney used the old trick of stuffing his camp bed with clothes and a pillow to make it look like he was sleeping inside. He took the sat nav from his bag, having previously entered the postcode of his secret rendezvous. He left a torch on a chair by his bed for when he returned, placing it on the glossy cover of his Edinburgh guide book. Then he crept to the end of the room, past all the camp beds and their sleeping occupants. Being such a warm night, all windows were open. He stood on a table and silently pulled himself up onto a ledge. He pushed the window fully open, slithered through onto the outside ledge and looked down into a small backyard, lit by flashing neon signs that pulsed across a row of wheelie bins. None of them were directly under the window so he had a long drop to the ground. He landed with a thud and crouched in the shadows until he was certain no one had seen or heard him. He could hear music in the street and the throbbing nightclubs beyond. Slowly he rose to his feet, clambered over a wall and slid out into the waiting night.

Chapter 22

The courtyard was bustling with young people laughing loudly, drinking and chattering in lively groups. Strings of coloured light bulbs danced on all sides from scaffolding where banners hung, with posters for stand-up shows that played long into the night and early hours. Floodlights shone through the branches and swaying foliage of a single tree, spilling down over table umbrellas marked 'Fosters', under which noisy students giggled round cluttered tables. The warm air was beery and raucous with friendly midnight banter.

Barney cast his eyes across the crowd. He felt uncomfortably conspicuous, not just because he was the only one by himself, but he was clearly the youngest for miles around. He walked self-consciously to the tree and stood in the comforting shadow of its trunk.

Blinking out through the floodlight, Barney spotted a familiar figure approaching. All he heard was a mumbled 'Follow me' as Seb walked on, disappeared behind a portacabin, then slipped down an alley, through a door, down a long corridor lined with posters and up a rickety wooden staircase. Barney ran to keep up, until Seb unlocked a door two floors up and entered a small bare room where a blanket hung in front of a window, a mattress lay on floorboards, clothes were draped over a suitcase and a dim light bulb dangled on a flex from a damp-stained ceiling. What looked like a bagged frame-tent was propped against the corner beside a laptop being charged on the floor.

"Welcome to my world." Seb smiled, closing the door behind them. "Coffee? Powdered milk, I'm afraid. I know it's a bit bleak but I'm only here for a few more days till I get something better. Have a seat." He pointed to the mattress, where Barney plonked down cross-legged.

Seb laughed. "Still the nimble little performer, I see!" He switched on a kettle standing on a stained patch of floorboard. "You managed to escape from your school party leader, then?"

"Just about," Barney said. "But if I get caught there'll be hell to pay."

"Sorry, Barney. It's just that I need to talk. I can't tell you how great it is to see you. Sorry about all that kerfuffle long ago with the hang-glider. I was given a hard time for leading you astray. You can see that I haven't given up trying to learn…" He pointed at the tall nylon bag in the corner. "I've got my own now. An eighteenth birthday present."

"I didn't tell Aries it was your idea to go flying, honest," Barney protested. "I refused to tell them anything. That's why I got thrown out, never to be used by your people again."

Seb stirred two mugs and handed one to Barney. "Sorry about the lumps." He spoke softly, with added seriousness. "I guess you heard about Tarquin?"

"He took an overdose, didn't he?"

"Not exactly." Seb sat beside Barney and lowered his voice to a faint whisper. "It's getting scary, I'm afraid. They've asked me to take over from Tarquin. He was on to something before Korova killed him. One fatal injection and straight in the river. That's why I have to keep watching my back. That's why I've had to bring you here secretly like this. Sorry about all the cloak and dagger stuff but it's to protect us both."

"I bumped into a couple of the terrorists at the Albert Hall a few months ago." Barney told him the whole story, including the hit and run van, and the bogus woman reporter.

Seb sat very quietly, deep in thought. "I'm sorry you've had that to deal with by yourself. It seems they've still got their eyes on you, then. I guess I shouldn't be telling you this, but I know I can trust you. Anyway, you should know in case…" He stopped whispering and got up to look outside the door. Then he turned off the light, pulled back the blanket and looked outside. With the light switched on again, Seb took a small device like a TV remote control from his bag. He pointed it to each wall and the ceiling.

"Just checking for listening devices. Looks like we're safe. Does the name Brigadier Dobson-Fowler mean anything to you?" Barney looked blank and shrugged as Seb continued. "No, it meant nothing to me, either. Apparently he was some bigwig in the armed forces a few years back. Some of his fellow officers informed on him to the government about his improper methods and he was sacked. All very messy and nasty. He was found guilty of brutal torture in Iraq and sent to prison. A real upper-crust bully, so the papers said. Apparently, ever since his release, he's been plotting revenge against his old military chums. It was Tarquin who discovered that this brigadier is behind Korova. We know they're plotting bomb attacks against military targets but, as yet, we don't know when or how. I was asked to come and sniff around as they think something is planned soon for round here. So far, that's all I know. A reliable source tells me the brigadier is also tied up with a company called Phipps Pharmaceuticals just down the road. So I'm currently trying to find out some inside info. I've got myself an interview tomorrow as a trainee lab technician at one of their many sites across the city."

Barney shuffled uneasily on the mattress. "Why are you telling me all this?"

"When I see you next, I'll tell you all I manage to find out. I sense this is bigger than MI5 realises. If anything happens to me before I can tip them the wink, I'd like you to rescue my memory stick." He pulled it from inside his shirt where it hung on a red strap like a medallion round his neck. "It's all on here. Round my neck. Make sure you get it – before they do. Is that OK?"

"Are you telling me you're working here by yourself?" Barney frowned.

"Afraid so. I've asked for reinforcements but they don't arrive till the weekend. Listen, I'd like to treat you to a decent bite to eat somewhere tomorrow night. How about it? Can you meet me again at the tree? Say ten o'clock?"

Barney thought. "I'll try. I'll have to tell a white lie to Mrs Peters. What's your phone number?"

"Hold on." Seb got a notepad and pencil. "Write yours on there and I'll write mine on here. Then we've got one minute to memorise each other's number before I set light to the paper. Ready?"

They completed the task, tested each other and burnt the paper within a minute, before they shook hands.

"I can't tell you what a relief it is to have someone nearby as back-up," Seb said. "But you'd best be getting back. I won't come out with you if you don't mind. I sensed I was followed earlier. Do you think you can find your way back?"

"I reckon so." Barney was already out of the door and descending the stairs. "I wish you'd tell the police."

"Yeah, soon. See you tomorrow."

Barney turned to wave and noticed the stress in Seb's eyes. Leaving the building, he walked through the floodlit courtyard still milling with students, then headed back along the street. With a quick bound over the wall, he was back beneath the window through which he'd climbed earlier. Except now it was different. One of the wheelie bins was exactly where he'd planned to move it so he could climb up more easily. *How strange that someone's already moved it*, he thought.

Clambering up to the window, Barney slid through deftly and lowered himself softly into the sighing room of heavy sleepers. He landed gently on the floor and squatted in the darkness before creeping along to the shadowy outline of his bed in the grey gloom. His hand reached to switch on his torch on the bedside chair, the sudden pool of light dazzling his eyes before he was able to see the familiar objects in front of him. Surprisingly, his guide book lay open, showing his name written inside. He was sure he had left it closed. But the biggest shock came when he turned and shone the beam onto his bed. For there in the middle, sticking up from what should have been his slumbering body, was a kitchen knife – its blade skewered right through to his mattress.

CHAPTER 23

ADVOCATE'S CLOSE, APARTMENT 4, EDINBURGH

The brigadier stood at the large dining room window, peering down over the city.

"Can't you just feel the history oozing out of every stone? This building is over four hundred and fifty years old, you know. I can almost smell the medieval."

"Don't I know it," Geoff grunted. "The drains stink. And you should hear the plumbing in the middle of the night. There's no lift, either. I must have lost three stone staggering up and down all these ruddy steps. Trust you to get this flat on the top floor."

"In a few days, we'll be making such colossal fortunes that you'll never have to walk up stairs again." He cast his eyes around the apartment. "As it is, it already appears that you do very little for yourself on the domestic front. Just as well I booked you your daily cleaner to come and keep the place free of vermin."

"I hardly see him. I'm often out when he comes. He doesn't speak a word of English."

"Maybe not," the brigadier said, snapping into his Commander-in-Chief role, "but make sure the briefing meeting agenda that I've just put on your table is kept out of sight. Clear? We need to keep watching our backs at all times. Complacency is our biggest enemy. Jan has already become careless. I understand she's taking sleeping tablets and medication for stress. I can't risk having a loose cannon in our midst. What is your assessment of her condition?"

Geoff sucked on a cigarette and pondered for a few seconds. "I like her. She's like me – rough as a badger's backside – but she's fearless. She speaks as she finds, just like me. You need someone who's scared of nothing. Your fancy Philippa, on the other hand, is a right gold digger and she's already got you round her pretty little finger – together with all the diamond rings you keep giving her." He blew out a string of smoke rings and waited for a reaction.

The brigadier's eyes narrowed threateningly. "I will not have Philippa's position questioned. She and Jan are in different leagues. They're chalk and cheese. Philippa is tall, slim, elegant and refined…"

"While Jan's short, fat and a nutcase? I still reckon she's OK."

"Very well, I will continue to monitor Jan's mental state but be prepared for my instruction to dispose of her in an instant should she become a liability. If need be, I will take on her duties myself if she cracks completely."

Geoff smiled. "Just remember, Brigadier, that they thought Edward Jenner was mad at first. Then they said he was a genius. Maybe Jan's the same – a bit of both."

The brigadier sighed and turned back to the window, his eyes scanning the miles of rooftops. "The ultimate irony is that Jenner was made a freeman of this very city, you know. The pioneering medical institutions here were key to eliminating the variola virus that was rife in the alleys and passageways below us. Millions died from festering pustules. Even as recently as nineteen forty-two, a deadly outbreak of smallpox struck this city. How bizarre that you and I will be responsible for putting the clock right back. Who knows, I may also become a freeman of this city when I offer my remedy for the scourge that's about to return with a vengeance."

Geoff slid back on the leather sofa, chewing thoughtfully. He pulled the gum from his teeth, rolled it into a slimy ball and posted it into an empty larger can, which he crumpled with one hand before hurling it at a litter basket. He missed.

"I'm not entirely sure what you're on about, Brigadier, but let's put it this way: in a couple of nights' time we'll be back up here to celebrate when it's all done and dusted. So if you'll excuse me, I'll just go and put the champagne on ice…"

Chapter 24

Laura was horrified. "A knife? Sticking out of your bed? What have you done with it?"

Barney looked around to make sure no one was within earshot before whispering, "I've hidden it in my bag. What else can I do? I can't exactly hand it to Mrs Peters and say, 'Oh, by the way, miss, this was sticking out of a pretend me when I sneaked out last night to meet a student MI5 agent who's up to his ears single-handedly trying to cock-up a Korova terrorist plot under our very own noses.' She'd have my father here in a shot to cart me off to the loony bin."

Laura raised her eyes in disbelief. "To be honest, I wouldn't blame her. Whatever are you gabbling on about? You're not making any sense, Barney. Who's the MI5 student? Are you making this up?"

"It's Seb. There's terrorist stuff going on round here and if that knife's anything to go by, I'm still a target."

"If you're not joking, this is scary, Barney." She looked at him anxiously. "I still don't know what you mean but you've got to tell someone. I couldn't bear to think of you getting hurt."

"I'm not that keen on getting hurt, either. Listen, I'm going to tell you everything I know about this Korova business and about Seb – on the condition you promise not to tell a soul. Then, if you're up for it, you might be able to help me. I could do with a bit of moral support and someone to stop me doing something crazy. But I really do understand if you want to keep well out if it. So, how about it? A pact or not?"

"Try me."

He told her everything. His dealings with MI5 – the full story.

"So on top of everything," he concluded, "by telling you all this, I've just broken the Official Secrets Act, but that's the least of my worries right now. So you see, it's because of all this Korova business that Greg was killed instead of me. That still upsets me. He'd have loved being up here with us in the show. I've been thinking about him a lot lately."

Laura said nothing as she struggled to make sense of what she'd just heard. "You mustn't sleep here tonight. It's too risky. Why don't you stay at your dad's to be on the safe side?"

"In case Knife Man returns? Yeah, maybe I will. That's a good idea. You see, that's why I need to have you involved. You're a lot more sensible than me. The thing is, I'm really concerned about Seb. He's in danger, too. Maybe he should stay at Dad's. I reckon Seb could do with our help, even if it's just to cheer him up a bit. I think he's well stressed-out. He'd like you, Laura."

There followed a long silence. "OK, count me in," she said after great thought. "What you've just told me sounds mad and utterly terrible but I can't get the sight of poor Greg and that van out of my head. If I can do something to get back at these Korova maniacs, then I must. It all sounds totally unbelievable but—"

"So you don't really believe me?" Barney interrupted sharply. "Then you'll have to join the queue. Everyone else thinks I've made it all up as well."

"No, you're right. Of course I believe you. It's just that all this takes a bit of getting my head round. So what's next? What do we do now? We've got to tell the police, surely."

"Yeah, that's what I told Seb. After tonight's show, I'll pop out to see him and we'll go to the police together. I'll tell Mrs Peters I'm meeting my dad for a meal. Then we'll just have to work out the best way of getting help and sorting everything out. I could do with you to keep Mrs Peters off my back."

Shortly before the evening show, Seb called Barney on his phone. Could he go straight to Seb's room where it would be safer to talk? Apparently there was much to say. It seemed going out for a meal was off. When Barney arrived at Seb's door, he knocked gingerly. He heard scuffling inside before a voice whispered, "Who is it?"

"It's Barney."

A key turned in the lock and the door quickly opened. "Come in, quick." Seb pulled Barney inside and locked the door behind him. "Come and sit down."

While Barney squatted on the mattress, Seb paced up and down, waving his arms and behaving very jittery.

"Calm down, Seb – you're a bit hyper tonight!"

"I know. I've found out something mind-boggling. It's so bizarre but I must run it by you. I was able to snoop around a bit today at Phipps Pharmaceuticals. Security was tight but I discovered something so scary, I've got to act fast. Luckily I got to chat-up a girl working at the labs and she gave a lot of information. I've yet to find out when, but I now know what, how and where."

Barney had no idea what Seb was saying but he knew it wasn't worth trying to interrupt his frenzied striding to and fro like a caged tiger.

"The thing is," he went on, "everything clicked into place when I saw the huge stocks of vaccine at the Phipps warehouse. Crates of the stuff. All this time we've assumed Korova's main mission is to attack the army. That's just a sideline – a smokescreen. The main clue is in the title!" He paused to see if Barney was keeping up.

"How's your Russian?" Seb asked.

"Er… pass."

"Mine isn't too hot either. I looked it up. Korova means cow. Vaccine comes from the Latin for cow – vacca. And who was the great scientist responsible for discovering vaccines derived from cows and cowpox? Edward Jenner. J1 is Jenner One. The first attack. There were boxes of them. Fireworks called 'Speckled Monsters'. And they're going to be let off in this very city very soon. And do you happen to know what Jenner meant by the 'speckled monster'?"

Barney frowned. "I think you've lost me with the cow bit."

"Smallpox. Barney, listen to me. Korova is engaged in bio-terrorism. That means they're going to release masses of the smallpox virus in the next firework display in this city. When people start dropping like flies, the stockpiles of the vaccine they've been mass-producing for years will be sold to the government for huge amounts of money. Look, I've checked the facts…" He read from his laptop screen.

"One: smallpox was the most feared highly infectious disease, killing an estimated three hundred million people worldwide in the last century alone.

"Two: smallpox is one of the most feared biological weapons because it is highly contagious as the virus can be spread very quickly through the air. It is difficult to treat, and the most dangerous strain can kill over one-third of those infected.

"Three: the virus once threatened sixty per cent of the planet, killing, scarring or blinding its victims. There was no cure but there was a vaccine – discovered by Edward Jenner in seventeen ninety-six in Gloucestershire when he injected a boy called James Phipps with cowpox that worked as a vaccine. It took until nineteen eighty to wipe out the disease worldwide.

"Four: everyone on the planet is now vulnerable to smallpox; vaccination throughout the world stopped well over thirty years ago, so no one is immune today."

He stopped to look at Barney, who gawped back, totally stunned. Seb squatted on the floor, sighed and continued very seriously. "The release of the virus from the sky would be undetected. The cloud of infection would be invisible, odourless, and tasteless. It would rain down on these streets and penetrate hundreds of buildings. No one would know until days or weeks later that anyone had been infected. Then all hell would be let loose. It's what's known as a pandemic – that's on a global scale. We're talking mega serious."

Barney muttered in disbelief. "We did smallpox in science. It was deadly, like the plague."

"Exactly," Seb continued, after peeping out through the window once more. "The smallpox virus, released in the sky in those 'speckled monster' fireworks I saw today, could survive for twenty-four hours in the open air, and will be highly infectious even at low doses. Hospitals just won't cope because the first victims would require rooms with special filters to stop the virus spreading through the air. Probably half the patients would die within days. Vaccines will be needed immediately for all health workers, then mass vaccination will be the only answer and guess what? No one makes the smallpox vaccine anymore. It will take three years before enough new supplies can be ready. The only outfit with the answer is Korova. They plan to sell each dose of vaccine for one hundred pounds. Multiply that by the millions of people in the country, not to mention around the world, and you see what huge money they'll make. They'll have the whole world by the throat – unless we stop them!"

"I'm sorry to ask this." Barney sounded very scared. "But how? Will the police, MI5 or whoever be able to catch them in time?"

"They'll have to. That's why I'm getting all the facts written up so I can get the lot to Aries. But I wish I could find out how long we've got. My guess is the Military Tattoo."

"Excuse me for asking, but what is the Military Tattoo, exactly?"

"I can tell you that. To be honest, I wasn't sure myself."

He tapped keys on his laptop. "It's a big show held every night up at the castle. Military bands and all that stuff. And at the end… ah, here it is…" He began quoting and, despite the seriousness of what he'd discovered, he couldn't help using his best Hollywood voice: "Now, the audience gather themselves together for the finale. All one thousand performers are on the Esplanade, column after column of marchers, dancers, and bandsmen. The audience joins in the great chorus of singing and cheering, and applause and cries of 'Bravo!' before a hush falls for the singing of the evening hymn, the sounding of the Last Post and the lowering of the flags. And finally, all eyes are drawn to the castle ramparts, where a single spotlight cues the lone piper to play his haunting lament, the high notes echoing across the still night sky and across the dark city, as the flames of the castle torchlights and the piper's warming brazier flicker and slowly die. Fireworks burst out against the black sky, but the spell is not broken for when we sing 'Auld Lang Syne' and shake our neighbour's hand, the emotions linger and the heart is full."

"Leaving the night chock-full of smallpox." Barney sighed. "So how do these special fireworks work, do you reckon?"

"I can tell you that because I examined one. There were boxes of them at the lab. They're just ordinary firework rockets but, at the bottom of the stick, a little upside-down test tube is attached. Just before they're let off, the stopper is taken off the test tube and whoosh… As the rocket flies, a jet of deadly fluid sprays across the sky. That way the virus doesn't get destroyed

173

by the heat of the rocket." Seb's eyes darted across his laptop screen. "It says here they don't do the fireworks every night. If we're lucky, it might not be till the end of the festival at the end of next week. But if not…"

"I still think you must tell the police or MI5 right now." Barney jumped to his feet.

"Hold on, Barney. I need to update one of my documents before I send it to Aries. I've been working flat-out all day but I'm nearly there. Tell you what, can you pop out and get me a sandwich from the courtyard? I haven't eaten all day. Here's a tenner. Cheese and pickle would be great but anything'll do. Get something for yourself too. When we've eaten, I'll encrypt my full report for sending – including these gross images of smallpox victims from the nineteen seventies. How could anyone dare to bring this back? It's totally sick."

He enlarged a picture of a girl smothered in angry blisters all over her face and body. Barney gasped in horror. "It looks like she's covered in baked beans. Poor kid – that's disgusting. You've got to stop this madness, Seb. You've put me off eating anything for a week but I'll go and get you something. You must be starving."

He went to the door as Seb took out a key and whispered agitatedly, "When you come back, knock six quick taps followed by a seventh after a pause." He unlocked the door to let Barney out. "Take care."

It felt so unreal walking out into a bustling floodlit courtyard where hundreds of people were relaxing, oblivious to the horrors of bio-terrorism immediately overhead. Somehow, queuing for a cheese and pickle sandwich with the imminent threat of smallpox seemed so pointless. Barney's impatience grew the longer he was kept waiting by trivial chatter of people around him, especially when various youths jostled past, jumping the queue to order drinks or plates of chilli. It took five minutes before Barney finally clutched in his hand a sealed plastic sandwich and a can of coke.

Dodging in and out of ticket queues, Barney eventually slipped behind the portacabin, down the alley, through the doorway and headed up to Seb's room. Halfway up the second flight of stairs, he stopped suddenly at a loud thud just above him. He looked up to see Seb staggering across the landing before slumping to his knees and falling across the top of the stairs. Footsteps ran away somewhere down a corridor. Barney ran to where Seb lay slouched against the wall, blood trickling from his mouth. He gurgled, staring straight at Barney as he tried to speak. "St… stick…" He pushed a scrap of crumpled, bloody paper into Barney's hand before grunting, tensing his fists, then falling limp. Barney felt for a heartbeat but pulled his hand away when he felt a spurt of warm blood. When he saw the memory stick was missing from round Seb's neck, the terrible truth finally struck him and he stared down in horror at Seb's grey, cold lips.

Barney stepped back, his stomach churning. It was then he saw the handle of a knife under Seb's body. Not thinking what he was doing, he pulled it out – as if removing it would somehow bring Seb back to life. But it didn't. Instead, mayhem broke loose. Two police officers came crashing up the stairs, shouting 'Freeze!'.

A camera flash blinded him as a woman officer commanded, "Put down the knife, son."

Barney was mumbling. "It's not what it looks like, honest. Seb was my friend." He felt tears spilling down his face and falling to the floor, where a squashed plastic-wrapped sandwich lay dripped with blood. He dropped the knife and stared at the police woman as he gabbled incoherently about terrorists with smallpox, vaccines, fireworks, MI5… Korova.

A firm hand grasped his arm. "What have you taken, son? How much?"

"I haven't stolen anything."

"I mean drugs. Or alcohol. How much?"

The other officer put a hand to Seb's neck. "Just caution the kid and arrest him. He's talking rubbish. It looks like we caught you literally red-handed, son. For once a tip-off was spot-on. Your fingerprints are all over the knife. You're under arrest."

"You've got to listen!" Barney was shouting now. "Whoever did this is one of the terrorists. You've got to stop them at the Tattoo…" He saw the glint of handcuffs as the woman tightened her grip on his arm. He was aware of a distant voice saying something about being under suspicion of murder and a whole gabble began spinning round his head.

"You do not have to say anything but it may harm your defence if you do not mention when questioned something which you later rely on in court. Anything you do say may be given in evidence."

The cold steel of the handcuffs touched Barney's wrists and he pulled away, yelling at the top of his voice,

"What part of *terrorist attack* don't you understand?" His mind flashed back to the first time he'd shouted that at a police officer in the school library. Months later they still weren't listening. In a sudden surge of renewed frustration he kicked the unopened coke can beside Seb's body. It flew past the officer's head, down the stairs and burst on impact against a wall.

The rest happened so quickly – just as the police lunged at him, trying to fasten the cuffs. A wave of panic and sheer desperation swept Barney off his feet, as he felt himself take off, without any idea what he was doing or where he was heading. With an impromptu display of bizarre gymnastics, he dived at the stair banister, slid part way down, then vaulted to the stairway below. He landed awkwardly by the still fizzing coke can and, with a similar manoeuvre, he leapt over that stair rail too. Now hurtling down the ground floor corridor, he plunged out through the door, with the police hot on his heels. He darted across the courtyard and out into the street, straight past the parked police car with its flashing blue light swirling into the night.

Dodging through traffic, diving down alleys and running instinctively back to base, he looked over his shoulder to make sure the police were nowhere to be seen before jumping over the back wall and crouching breathlessly among the wheelie bins. Only then, sweating, shivering and desperate to be sick, did he look at the scrunched paper in his bloody hand. In the darkness and with a throbbing head, he couldn't make sense of the few letters and numbers scrawled there, so he stuffed it in his pocket and reached for his phone. It was time to call for help. But it was only as he scrolled through his contacts that he realised the dreadful truth. No one could help him now.

CHAPTER 25

Squatting in deep dark shadows between wheelie bins, as a pulsing blue light swept around him, Barney could only lie low and wait, not daring to stir. By now Mrs Peters would have reported him as missing and it wouldn't take long for the police to realise the absconded schoolboy was the killer they were hunting. They were bound to search his belongings and find the knife from the night before – and leap to all kinds of conclusions. He knew it would be hopeless trying to talk himself out of this.

When at last the blue light moved on, Barney tried to think more calmly. There was no one he could phone. It was past one o'clock on Saturday morning, he was being hunted by a gang of terrorists, the police and probably a furious Mrs Peters. He needed to warn the security services urgently but he had no contact number. Phoning his dad would be pointless as there would be a massive row, his mum would go berserk and his gran would worry all night. So he'd just have to wait until the morning and try to talk to Laura then. This would be a very long and lonely night.

It was impossible for Barney to sleep, although occasionally he dozed for just a few seconds, drifting into a semi-conscious nightmare. Each time he came to with a start, his mind was in a whirl of confusion. The real nightmare was almost as bad as the horrors in his delirium. The terrifying images in his head just wouldn't go away and he could no longer think clearly. Seb was his friend and he couldn't really be dead.

Barney's mind flashed back to the image of Greg lying crumpled in the road. In all those dreams since, Greg had jumped up again and ran off, like in cartoons. For weeks Barney expected to see Greg walk in through the door with no more than a few bruises. Even now, he sometimes wondered if Greg would turn up to watch the show or maybe Seb would come to watch again after being revived in hospital. Then they'd meet afterwards for that meal he promised and they'd laugh again. Laughter suddenly filled his head as a group of late night revellers walked past. Barney opened his eyes with a start. *Will I ever be able to laugh again?*

Eventually, after hours of torture, Barney reached for his phone. The sky was becoming lighter and somewhere in the distance he heard birds twittering. Unlikely though it was that Laura's phone would be switched on, he pressed the key and almost instantly heard her voice.

"Barney, where are you?"

"Laura, you're awake." It was an absurd thing to say but he wasn't thinking straight.

"I've been awake all night, waiting for you to call. Thank God you're safe. I'm under strict instructions to get Mrs Peters the second you call, but of course I won't. The police were here. They've taken away a lot of your stuff. I managed to rescue your sat nav, but that's about all, I'm afraid."

"Laura, listen. I need the wig I wear on stage. And can I borrow your jacket with the hood? I need dark glasses.

Anything to disguise myself. Laura, I didn't do it, honest. They killed Seb."

"Barney, of course you're innocent! I tried to tell the police everything when they were interviewing us all – but I could tell they thought I was a nutcase. Mrs Peters told me off for being hysterical and got all stressy and said, 'There must have been some terrible mistake.' They told me I'd been watching too much fantasy rubbish. But never mind me – where are you?"

"Sitting by the wheelie bins round the back. It's freezing. But I need to get away from here. I keep thinking about Seb. He was such a nice guy and didn't deserve this. He discovered loads of scary stuff that I must pass on but I don't know where I can go. Everyone wants me locked up. Laura, it's hopeless."

"No it isn't, Barney. I think you're great. We'll sort this. I'll be there in a minute."

As he switched off his phone, he saw the screwed up paper smeared with dried blood still in his hand. However much he stared at it, the letters failed to make any sense at all. It looked like SdIIH3. Maybe it was a car number plate. Was it a code? Whatever it meant, Barney was sure it must have been important to Seb. It was his dying message to the world, after all.

Reassured by Laura's voice, Barney slipped into a peaceful doze and the next thing he knew was Laura hugging him.

"Am I pleased to see you!" she said. "Sorry I've been so long but I've written a note for Mrs Peters. I told her I'm out looking for you and I'll be back soon. I don't want her sending the police after me as well. Right, here are some things for you. I got you some real glasses rather than sunglasses. Not many people wear those at six in the morning! Stay still – time for some adjustment. To match the black wig."

She carefully darkened his eyebrows with a stick of stage make-up. "There, with that wig, hood and glasses, even your own mum wouldn't recognise you."

"I bet Gran would!"

"That's more like it – you managed a smile. Come on, we need to get away from here. Let's find somewhere for some breakfast where we can talk." She led him by the arm along the empty street. They paused at a newsagent where the morning's papers were being displayed on a rack. The headline: '**Boy Killer on the Loose**' glared up at them, with a picture of Barney's startled face filling the front page. They stood in silence as they scanned the first sentences, before Laura pulled away.

"I don't think we need to look at this," she said. They walked on, saying nothing, each lost in their own troubled thoughts. Although they passed very few people, it seemed everyone was staring suspiciously and reaching for their phones.

"Hey, this place looks open." They tumbled into a grubby-looking café where clouds of steam and throaty hisses rose from an urn. A woman in an apron was wiping tables and singing along to a radio. She sounded Spanish.

"Hi, kids. I be with you soon."

They chose a table at the back, well away from the window. As soon as he sat down, Barney poured out the whole story of the night before. Laura listened in disbelief at Korova's plot to infect people with smallpox. Even the arrival of mugs of tea and a plate of steaming chips did little to lift their spirits.

Barney stared into his mug as if the answer to all his troubles was swirling round inside. "I really liked Seb. He was a good bloke. He so didn't deserve to die like that. I'm determined to find his memory stick because that was the last thing he tried to tell me. His killer had wrenched it from his neck so the only thing to go on is this…" Barney showed Laura the paper with the strange code: SdIIH3.

"I wish it could mean something." He thumped the table and spilt the tea. "If it could help me find that memory stick, I'd be able to use it to convince the police and MI5 to act fast. I reckon we've got a week at the most. They probably let the fireworks off a week tonight at the end of the festival. I've got a week to prove everything – that's if I don't get arrested and spend forever in a police cell."

Laura examined the letters on the paper. "If it's a postcode, maybe Seb was trying to tell you where his killer lives. Try it in your sat nav just in case."

"I'd already thought of that, but that's not a proper postcode. My sat nav can't come up with an address."

"More tea? I have more in pot." The woman put a teapot on the table. She was about to move the piece of paper when Laura snatched it away and looked at it upside-down.

"Try putting this in your sat nav. Maybe we've been looking at it the wrong way up. Try EH1 1PS."

He tapped it in.

"Blimey, you're right!" Barney's face lit up. "It says it's a place called Advocate's Close and it's not far from here. I reckon it's worth going to have a look, at least."

Laura's face said it all – she feared things could get even scarier. "I guess it's a risk we've got to take."

Although it was still early on Saturday morning, The Royal Mile was already beginning to bustle with tourists. Barney's sat nav tingled his fingers and led them towards the castle. Then it twitched and steered them off the main street, under an arch and down steps to a dark passage with ancient walls towering up on both sides.

Barney stared up at windows high above them. "Those must be flats but how do we get up there?" After walking down steps and alleys, they emerged at the other side of the building where there was an entrance behind tall railings. Once through a squeaking iron gate, they pushed open the door and peered inside. Leading up from a gloomy entrance hall, a flight of stairs twisted its way to landings far above.

"It would be a lot easier if we knew which number we're looking for," Laura said.

They began climbing, passing a man in a fluorescent jacket, whistling as he read electricity meters in a cupboard, before they eventually reached the very top landing with a row of blue front doors facing them. At the far end, a man in a dustcoat was clattering about in a small utility room. He emerged with a vacuum cleaner, a steaming bucket and a mop.

"Hi there, it very nice day I thinks," he said in broken English, before going to one of the doors, producing a key and letting himself inside.

"I wonder if he might be able to help us," Laura said. "Let's wait in his cleaning room and talk to him when he comes back. He seems cheerful enough."

They sneaked into the small room to wait beside a gurgling sink, a rumbling tumble dryer and an array of brooms.

"This is hopeless." Barney sighed. "It's like looking for an invisible needle in an imaginary haystack."

"Quick, pull the door shut, there's someone out there." Laura peeped out through a narrow gap. It was a postman knocking at a front door. They heard his cheery voice echo around the landing.

"Good morning. Nice bright day. There's a package for you to sign for."

The reply sounded much grumpier. "You woke me up. I was having a lie-in."

Barney's eyes opened wide. "Let me look." He peered out and blurted in a loud whisper, "That's him! It's Australia Head. I'd know that voice and face anywhere. That's the flat we want."

"I don't think 'want' is quite the right word. But it's probably where we need to search for Seb's memory stick. I don't fancy getting caught by him." Laura stared at his mean eyes and blotchy face while Barney's brain buzzed with bizarre plans.

"Somehow we've got to get him out of there. If I could get inside for a few minutes to snoop around, you could keep watch outside and warn me if anyone comes."

Laura was still trying to come up with a better suggestion when the man in the dustcoat reappeared, clunking his way along the landing. He stopped at Australia Head's door and knocked. It took a while for it to open.

"Ah, Mr Geoff. I clean, yes?"

"Is it impossible to have a decent lie-in these days? Can't you do somewhere else first? Tell you what, go and get me a newspaper."

"Sorry, Mr Geoff. I no understand."

"Come back in ten minutes." He held up his fingers and thumbs and pointed at his watch. "Ten minutes. Forget it. Do my kitchen and I'll get the blasted paper myself."

Both men went inside and the door closed again. "We might be in luck. Listen, Laura – if Australia Head goes out, you could try to distract the cleaner and I'll slip inside. Then you could hide in that electric cupboard where we saw the meter reader and phone me when Australia Head comes back. That will give me a minute to get out and sneak in here again. What do you think?"

"Sounds great but what if… Hey, look, he's just come out. Australia Head's going down the stairs. Quick, hide somewhere!"

She ran to the front door and knocked. Barney sneaked down a few stairs as the cleaner opened the door. "Hi. Mr Geoff just go out…"

"No, it's you I want. I think there's a leak in that room. Can I show you?" She beckoned him towards the utility room.

"What is leak?"

As soon as the man was far enough away, Barney ran back up and slipped through the open front door. Once inside, he dashed into each room in a desperate search for a laptop or memory stick. He was looking at papers strewn across a bed when the cleaner returned, so Barney darted inside a fitted wardrobe and slid the door shut. He stood very still inside while the vacuum cleaner droned in the next room.

Laura ran down flights of stairs until she came to the meter cupboard. It was just big enough for her to squeeze inside, pull the door closed and peer out through the wooden slats. She could see the stairs clearly as she remained motionless at her lookout post. With her phone clutched in her hand, at the ready, she waited as the meters whirred in her ear.

Barney slid back the wardrobe door when he heard the cleaner rattling his bucket on the landing and shutting the front door. The apartment fell eerily silent as it filled with the strong smell of pine disinfectant. A warm breeze blew in from a large open window where Barney briefly paused by fluttering curtains to look out over a narrow balcony, big enough only for a few pots of geraniums. He crept away to search through each room, his pulse quickening and his clammy hands tingling. He only had a minute if he was lucky, but there was no memory stick to be seen. Dashing across the kitchen, he slipped on wet tiles and clattered into a table where envelopes lay unopened. Beside them was the recently delivered package containing several sinister-looking syringes. Underneath was a front door key, which he slipped into his pocket. A printed sheet of A4 caught his eye, with the heading:

Final Briefing Meeting: J1
Clarence Hotel – Room 42
Saturday @ 1800 hours. BE PUNCTUAL

Barney didn't stop to read the details printed underneath but snatched up the paper, folded it hurriedly and stuffed it in his back pocket. He checked his phone to make sure there were no calls, before searching the drawers of a cluttered desk.

Laura heard heavy footsteps on the stairs beside her and glimpsed grubby jogging-bottoms move past, climbing each step with solid plods. She quickly pressed her phone to send the alarm. Her gasp was audible when she saw with horror the message flash: '**No signal**'. She tried again, then again, but her phone refused to send the warning.

Barney, oblivious to her efforts and of the breathless man now approaching the top of the stairs, continued rummaging through a drawer – until he heard a key turning in the lock. He looked up in panic and slid the drawer shut. His eyes darted around the room for a place to hide. Nowhere. The front door opened as Barney scuttled across the room towards the billowing curtains at the open window. It was a crazy idea, but there was nowhere else to hide. He crawled out onto the tiny balcony crammed with pots and he stood rigidly at the very edge with his back pressed against the wall, his waist pushing into the iron rail at his side. He peered over at the sheer drop to the concrete path many floors below, with its railings pointing up at him like taunting spears. He sighed and closed his eyes at his stupidity of ending up out here – from frying pan to fire.

Suddenly the window at his shoulder rattled and a voice in his ear grumbled, "Damn that cleaner. Blooming draft." The window slid down with a firm clunk and the catch snapped shut. Locked. Barney's first feeling was one of relief at not being discovered – yet. But then the awful truth faced him. He was stuck five floors up on a great cliff of a building, with no way of getting back inside. Below him, people moved like ants along the path. He remained very still, not looking down but staring out across the roofs and spires, the city sounds blowing up to him on a warm boisterous wind.

After minutes of standing like a statue and cursing Laura for not phoning the alarm, Barney was still trying to think what he could do. One thing was certain – he couldn't risk being seen from inside the window. The man in there would hurl him to his death in seconds. One shove from his thick arms and Barney would plunge, to be skewered on the railings below. But the alternative was almost as scary. Somehow, he would have to climb down. Once more he peered down but it was hopeless. Even an experienced rock climber would tremble at the prospect. He leaned over to get a better look, as the soles of his feet prickled and his armpits burned.

The only other narrow balcony was two floors below, further along the wall. Barney's crazy idea was to get there – in some way or other . At least the occupant of that apartment wasn't likely to kill him, even though his

189

attempt to get to it might. Sticking out a few centimetres from the wall of the apartment below was an overflow pipe. Maybe, just maybe, it would take his weight.

Barney gripped the rail beside him and flipped over, his legs swinging under the balcony in a rush of air. His hands slid down the rails to the balcony base, his legs now dangling over nothingness – just a sheer drop to solid cement spiked with iron railings.

He tried to swing his legs so he could drop at an angle. Never had he imagined in his gym training that his life would depend on his skills learned on the parallel bars and vaulting horse. A noise at the window above made him let go sooner than he'd intended. He fell, scraping across the rough wall and grazing his cheek as he grabbed at the overflow pipe. It bent and cracked but held, as a chunk of brick flew out into mid-air before clunking on the railings below. Looking down through his swinging feet, he could just see the balcony below as the pipe in his hands was working loose. He tried to work up a momentum, swinging to and fro, like on a trapeze. With one more push he swung forwards and the pipe snapped. He swung across the wall, scraping his elbow as he grabbed at the balcony rail rushing up at him. His arms wrenched, his wrists twisted and his fingers locked, but he held on for dear life.

Having held his breath during the whole manoeuvre, Barney began to breathe again, panting and spluttering as he pushed his feet against the wall and began walking up the bricks to get a toehold on the balcony floor. Hauling himself up and breathlessly clambering over the railings, he dropped to his knees beside a growbag of tomato plants on the small balcony. For a few seconds he lay on his back, staring up at the blue sky, and he smiled. To his relief, the window was open slightly so he lifted it enough to slide through into the soothing stillness of an elegant sitting room. With adrenaline still pumping and his t-shirt drenched with sweat, Barney stood among polished antique furniture and potted palms. He crept over thick carpet to a doorway and peered into the hall, with a front door at the far end – the way out of his nightmare.

Suddenly aware of a woman singing in the shower in the room beside him, Barney crept past and reached out to open the front door – just as the bathroom door behind him opened. A large middle-aged woman stepped out, wrapped in a towel. She screamed as he pulled open the door, muttered, "Very sorry, madam," and ran out onto the landing. Even after he'd darted down a full flight of stairs, he could still hear the woman shouting behind him.

"Help, there's a peeping tom on the loose – in a wig!"

It was only then he realised the wig had slipped and his glasses were missing. They must have flown off as he'd grazed his ear while flying across the building. Despite his odd appearance, someone still recognised him when he reached the ground floor.

"Barney!" Laura flung her arms round him. "Am I glad to see you! I tried to phone you but—"

"I thought you'd abandoned me." He smiled. "I'm a tad pleased to see you too! I'll tell you about it when we can get off the street and find somewhere safe. No memory stick, I'm afraid, but I did find this." He took out the folded paper from his back pocket.

"They're having a meeting today at the Clarence Hotel in room 42 and this is what it says – look."

Laura read it.

Agenda: Final timing & duties/responsibilities
Fireworks: Arthur's Seat/Castle
TATP: coach
Debrief meeting & contingency planning

"So it looks like we've got an appointment at eighteen hundred hours," Barney went on. "At the Clarence Hotel, wherever that is."

Laura took his arm and led him out into the dazzling sunlight. "Then we'll just have to find out."

They stood beside shiny black railings, feeling the warm sun on their faces. Barney reached up and lifted his glasses off a pointed iron prong where they were bayoneted. He didn't dare squint up at the balcony to relive his ordeal, but instead looked down at the slabs at his feet. He said nothing but thought how easily he could have ended up splattered right there... or a broken mess impaled for all to see on those ornate sunlit spikes. It didn't bear thinking about – especially with the next unimaginable challenge just hours away.

CHAPTER 26

The heavy church door shut with a clunk that echoed around the musty interior. After the noise of the streets, the silence inside seemed stifling, but also comfortingly safe as a temporary refuge. Apart from a woman arranging flowers on a pedestal near the altar, the church was empty. She looked up and smiled before returning to a bucket of white lilies as Barney and Laura shuffled behind a pillar and sat on a pew that creaked beneath them.

"I've switched my phone off," Laura whispered. "Mrs Peters keeps trying to get me. I can almost hear her screaming."

"It's best not to use our phones at all in case they can trace where we are," Barney said, just as the door behind them clunked open. He quickly knelt on the floor, resting his elbows on the pew in front and cupping his hands over his face, as if in deepest prayer. Laura followed suit as footsteps passed down the aisle nearby. Peeping out between his fingers, Barney watched a priest talking to the flower arranger and glancing in his direction. His fingers quickly covered his eyes once more and his prayer-pose continued until he felt Laura digging him in the ribs.

"You were asleep." She smiled. "It's OK, they've gone. We're alone in here now. Chillax."

"That's just what I was doing. I was zonked out!"

"I thought you were praying for help."

Barney sat back on the pew. "Funny you should say that. I'm not religious or anything but I said a few words for Seb. I can't get him out of my mind."

"There are some candles over there. Why don't you light one for him? I think I'll light one for Greg."

Without saying more, they slowly stood and, as the pew creaked again in the cool stillness, they crept to the altar steps where they knelt by a cluster of unlit candles and a box of matches. They each struck a match and stared thoughtfully as the two wicks flickered to life in front of them.

"If there's a God," Barney said, the flames dancing in his eyes, "I hope we'll get a bit of help today. Let's face it, we've got an impossible task on our own."

Laura stood and looked around at the marble figures and stained glass windows. She took a postcard from a bookcase below an ornate brass plaque on the wall and dropped a coin in the collection box. "I'll get you a souvenir. Listen, we've still got a few hours before we need to be at the Clarence Hotel. If we can lie low here till then, we might get a bit of sleep. I feel as shattered as you look. There's a side chapel round there. How about it?"

They both crawled under the little altar table and lay on the carpet beneath. With the altar cloth reaching the floor on all sides, they were hidden inside a snug dark tent. They lay looking up at the underside of the table, each wrapped in their own thoughts and fears.

"I'd never thought about dying before," Barney whispered. "I've seen two bodies now. Both killed suddenly and horribly. I could be the next victim… or of smallpox." He turned his head to look into Laura's eyes. "Please take care, won't you? I couldn't bear it if you got hurt or if…"

"We've got to be positive." She squeezed his hand and pushed the postcard into it. "Keep this in your pocket. It's got a picture and a few words. It might help." They lay in silence for a long time before she said, "Are you asleep?"

"No. I can't sleep. I've never felt so tired, though."

"Me too. What are you thinking?"

"Lots. About Seb. About us. About today. About Mum. About Gran."

"How is she now?"

"Still having tests. If she goes into hospital, I might live with Dad for a while. I might have to anyway if Mum marries Owen. This weekend they're going away to 'discuss their future'. I really don't mean to upset her but he's so rubbish. He treats me like I'm five and only talks to me about rugby. Mum says I'm selfish and I've got to try harder to like him."

"I'd hate it if you moved away, Barney. It would be terrible. Besides, look what excitement I'd miss!"

"I'd hate it, too. I'd miss you loads. Living with Dad could be a problem. I just wish I could prove to him I'm not a complete waste of space. If only I could make him feel proud of me for once."

"I'm proud of you, Barney. I never realised all that Korova stuff was going on and you've had to keep it all to yourself for so long. You're amazing."

"Cheers, Laura. Apart from Gran, you're the only one in the entire universe who's ever said that."

"Mrs Rickman likes you lots. She told me she thinks you're adorable."

"Good old Mrs Rickman. Without her play to keep me going, I'd have gone mad."

Their whispers fell silent again as they lay very still in the darkness, listening to their own breathing and the slow tock of a clock in the tower. Before long they were both asleep and lost in the far more comforting world of their dreams.

Voices. Music. They woke suddenly to a blast from the organ. The space in which they lay seemed to explode with a deep rumble and stirring chords from the organ pipes just metres away. Barney sat up and cracked his head on the table. He squinted at his watch for several seconds before he could make out the time.

"Blimey, it's gone half past three. We'd better get going."

"Then you'd better get your sat nav switched on to lead us to the hotel. But the only trouble is…" Laura lifted the altar cloth and peered out into the church. "There's some kind of service going on. There's a choir walking down the aisle. It looks like a wedding. I'm trying to see if I can see the wedding dress."

"Laura, what are you like? What is it with girls and wedding dresses? Is this really the time to be admiring a wedding dress?"

"Yes," she giggled. "It could be our way to escape. To get out without being seen we might have to hide under it!"

Chapter 27

Jenners Department Store, Edinburgh

"How about a pot of Lapsang Souchong tea?" The brigadier lifted a tray from the rack and slid it towards the till.

"Lap what?"

"Never mind." He sighed disdainfully. "No doubt you'd prefer PG Tips and a pink fairy cake to match that thing through your eyebrow."

Jan ignored him and peered through the glass at a caramel slice. "I'll stick to black coffee. It'll keep my mind alert for the task ahead."

His frown said it all. "Let's hope it sobers you up," he mumbled. They sat by a window and both glanced down into Princes Street, saying nothing over the chinking of china and rattle of spoons. "I'm sure the significance of this establishment hasn't escaped you, Jan," he said at last, squeezing a wedge of lemon into his cup.

"Your tea smells like old kippers," she sneered. "How do you mean, exactly?"

"The name, my dear – Jenners. Just the job."

She tutted and rolled her eyes. "Don't you think of anything else? You're totally obsessed. I wouldn't be surprised if you've got obsessive compulsive disorder."

He glared at her frostily. "You are not my prison warden any longer. I would remind you I am in charge now and I have every reason and right to be obsessive. I call it being totally focused. I know my mind. A place with this name is where you, in particular, need to concentrate on the brink of our mission."

"Seems a bit superstitious to me," she said.

He crossly slammed his lemon wedge on the table. "Nonsense. I am perfectly rational and focused, with a professional scientific mind; rather that than being mentally unstable under stress."

Jan dropped a sugar lump into her coffee and glowered. "I am not mentally unstable. I'll have you know I'm in complete control, despite what you all think of me. I'm sick of everyone accusing me of buckling under the pressure. I made a mistake about that boy, that's all. I admit it. Why can't we all move on?"

"Because you were meant to kill him and he's still out there. You failed at Operation Roadkill and you couldn't even kill the boy in his bed the other night. I would have thought murdering a sleeping child in a church hall would be a piece of cake. Now he's all over the newspapers when he should have been silenced. Had you kidnapped him the first time you met him as instructed, none of this would have happened. To me, that smacks of incompetence."

Her neck and cheeks reddened. Even her fiery deep-set eyes were red-rimmed.

"All right, all right. Stop bleating on about the kid. He's no longer a problem. You have my word. I guarantee he won't bother us." She couldn't disguise the tension and mounting anger in her voice.

"You need a break, my dear. It's just as well your work will soon be finished."

"I am not cracking!" she shouted above the hushed conversations around them.

"Keep your voice down, you fool." He blew on his cup and took a small sip as they sat in strained silence. He looked at his watch. "Just six hours to blast-off. Thousands of people will be out there tonight, all packed together, expecting the display of a lifetime... and Geoff will give it to them. His Speckled Monsters will swoop over them and drizzle the deadly contents for mass-inhalation, then mass annihilation. How very satisfying. It's perfect weather, too. Warm and breezy. The virus will spread like wild fire."

"Your beloved Geoff never fails," she muttered sulkily.

"He's professional," he barked. "Just like you used to be. Just like you are about to be again. I don't want you falling at the last hurdle. You must keep away from alcohol, too."

"That's my business," she snapped, with an angry clatter of cup and saucer.

"Not if it affects your work." His venomous whisper and savage eyes were full of menace. "If I can't trust you, Jan, I will have to do the job myself and adjust your final payment accordingly."

She struggled to keep control as the brigadier stared in unnerving silence before adding, "Your final task is essential in bringing this city to a grinding halt. You have the fireworks in the boot of your car?"

"Of course. All primed and ready."

"You know the exact grid reference?"

"Trust me. I'll be on the cliff under Arthur's Seat in good time. On the dot of twenty-two hundred hours I'll release the lot."

"The direction is vital. You must point them all at the Parliament Building. I want every politician infected when they arrive for work. You must also target Holyrood Palace where the Royals are about to visit. You have the most virulent strain in those test tubes. Just as well you're now fully vaccinated. The virus will remain live for days provided it keeps cool."

"Don't worry. They're in a cool box. I won't let you down. I'll be at the top of the cliff in good time. I'll make my way up there straight after our meeting."

"That's my girl, Jan."

"Don't patronise me. I'm not your precious Philippa who can never put a foot wrong. She gets paid double for half the work just because she's your fancy-woman. You've never liked me because I talk to you frankly – and I haven't got legs like hers."

The brigadier drained his cup and dabbed a paper napkin over his lips. "Come now, my dear. We don't want jealousy to cloud our thinking and upset working relationships. I brought you here to reassure you of how important you are and how, at midnight tonight, you will be a very rich woman. Should you administer your duties successfully, I'll be only too happy to write your cheque with an extra zero added – as a special bonus."

She looked up and managed to smile for the first time. "Nice coffee," she said.

CHAPTER 28

The foyer at the Clarence Hotel was a commotion of arrivals and departures, with queues at the reception desk, staff bustling in all directions and luggage trolleys whirling to and from waiting taxis.

"The secret is to look *chillaxed*, like we know exactly what we're doing," Barney whispered from the corner of his mouth, while peering into the hotel entrance from the pavement outside.

"Yeah, let's make sure we look better than we did crawling from under the table at that church. I've never felt so embarrassed with everyone staring at us. At least you've got that wig to disguise yourself. I won't be able to show my face near there again." Laura just managed to avoid a case on wheels trundling past, pulled by an elderly woman in a black shawl, high heels and a face thick with powder.

"Wow, that was close." She laughed. "I nearly got flattened by a granny wagon. Anyway, what is it exactly we're trying to do here?"

"Not sure – apart from finding room forty-two. If we can get hard evidence and details, I might be able to convince the police. At least we're here early enough to snoop around before the meeting."

"What are we snooping for?"

"No idea – till we find something useful."

"Right," Laura began assertively. "We need a story –

why we are here. Let's say we're brother and sister come to meet our uncle from America. Uncle Chuck."

Barney laughed. "Yeah, and if we're not careful, that's what they'll do – chuck us out."

Laura pointed through the glass doors. "If we sit on that sofa in the foyer and act all casual, we can then work out how to get to room forty-two and see what security's like."

The automatic doors glided open and they strolled in, acting like they'd been there hundreds of times before. They approached the sofa and sat down, casually glancing around as a porter stared at them, somewhat suspiciously. Barney spoke into his phone.

"Hi, Uncle Chuck. We're in reception… great." He turned to Laura. "He says he'll be down in five minutes."

The porter seemed satisfied and left them alone. Laura's eyes fixed on a woman with a pink ponytail and a red top with tassels. Having checked in, the woman was given a key with a magnetic strip, which she swiped at a door. It clicked open and she walked through, down a corridor towards a lift. The security door sprung shut and locked firmly again.

"How do we get through there, then?" Laura mouthed discreetly. "It's the only way to get to the rooms inside. We'll need a key."

"Leave it to me." Barney's ventriloquism stopped abruptly as he watched the elderly woman with shawl, high heels, powdered face and a very loud bossy voice, fumbling in her handbag at the desk.

"Can you order me a taxi?" she barked at the receptionist. "I'm meeting a friend at the Usher Hall for tea before the concert. I'll be back at about ten o'clock, if you could have a little light supper brought to my room on a tray then. Nothing spicy."

The receptionist tried to smile politely. "Certainly, madam. What is your room number?"

"I have no idea. I suppose it's on my key." She fumbled once more, the black silky shawl slipping off her shoulder to the floor. "I knew I should have pinned the darn thing. Now then, here's the key. What does that say? I haven't got my glasses."

"Three-one-nine, madam. A taxi is waiting outside for you."

"Splendid." She dropped the key into her bag and tottered to the main door, brushing past the sofa where Barney sat with his arm stretched across the headrest. With the slightest movement of his fingers, he tweaked the woman's shawl as she walked past and it slid to the floor once more. Barney leapt to his feet, scooped up the shawl and ran over to her as she approached the door.

"I believe you dropped this," he said.

"What? Oh darn the thing. It keeps slipping off. Just stuff it in my bag. I'll sort it out in the taxi. Thank you, young man." She wobbled on her heels through the door, waving at a taxi, as Barney returned to the sofa unable to hide his grin.

"What was all that about?" Laura asked. "Since when have you been such a gentleman?"

"Since I realised we needed a key." He opened his hand to reveal the key to room 319. "So would you like to accompany me into the hotel, young lady?" He smiled.

"I should be delighted, you clever little pickpocket!"

"Not pocket. Handbag, actually."

When the porter was safely out of sight, they walked confidently to the locked door and gave a single swipe of the tab. With a buzz and a click, the door unlocked, letting them enter the secure corridors beyond, before it slammed shut behind them. A woman in an overall looked at them warily from a cleaning cupboard but she said nothing. They ran past and upstairs to the next floor where they found room 42. The door was slightly open so Barney pushed it and peered inside. The lights were switched off and the empty room was gloomily quiet. Enough light seeped through the closed blinds at the window to show a round table surrounded by blue plastic chairs. A flip chart stood in the corner, so this was clearly a room for meetings. Five places were set with leather writing folders around the table, with glasses and bottles of water in the centre.

Laura looked at her watch. "In ten minutes they'll be in here. Oh to be a fly on the wall and be able to listen to everything."

"We'll have to do the next best thing," Barney said, taking out his phone and the folded paper from his pocket. "It mentions here Arthur's Seat. Where is that exactly?"

"I think it's a hill near here. I'll Google it." She searched on her phone and read aloud, "Arthur's Seat is the main peak of hills which form Holyrood Park, a wild piece of highland landscape in the city of Edinburgh, about a mile to the east of Edinburgh Castle. Though it can be climbed from almost any direction, the easiest ascent is from the east. However, each year people fall to their deaths from the top of Salisbury Crags. The hill above the cliff has caught fire in dry summers or on Guy Fawkes Night due to stray fireworks, when the fire brigade has tackled blazes for many hours." She switched off her phone while Barney thought aloud.

"So it seems like they're planning something for there as well, then. It's vital we hear what they're about to discuss." He stood on a chair and pushed up one of the tiles in the suspended ceiling. "This is the only thing I can think of," he said, switching on his phone. "It'll use up all our call time but it could be worth it. Just call my number."

Laura switched her phone back on, scrolled to 'Barney' and pressed 'call'. When his phone bleeped, he answered and posted it up through the gap in the ceiling directly above the table. He lowered the tile again and sat on the chair. "Can you go outside and listen on your phone and tell me if you can hear what I'm saying?"

Out in the corridor Laura could just hear Barney's muffled voice through her phone. Enough to make out a nursery rhyme. She poked her head back through the door. "'Twinkle Twinkle Little Star', by any chance?"

"Spot on. Brilliant. Now all we have to do is listen from the safety of room three-one-nine."

They took the lift up two more floors and used the woman's key to enter room 319.

Barney sat on the bed and held Laura's phone to his ear. "I can hear someone talking down there." It was the brigadier.

"This is the evening I have been waiting for at last." His voice was barely audible at first. After Laura turned up the volume to maximum and switched to speakerphone, they could hear the sound of water being poured into a glass followed by more voices.

"Let's hope no one's late," Philippa said, glancing at her bracelet-watch.

The brigadier sounded on edge. "Precisely, Philippa. We start in four minutes, regardless. Timing is key. I chose to meet here rather than at the apartment because the underground parking here is nice and cool. I couldn't risk leaving vehicles out there in direct sunlight with those precious fireworks in the car boots."

Although much of the talking that followed was unclear, Barney could discern different yet scarily familiar voices. Australia Head had arrived, the man with the squint and the woman with the eyebrow ring. Suddenly there was banging on the desk.

"Ladies and gentlemen," the brigadier began. "Close the door and sit down. Firstly, we must synchronise our watches. It is now eighteen hundred hours precisely. Our timing tonight is crucial. In the unlikely event that tonight's J1 operation has to be aborted, we have next Saturday as a final reserve. As you know, I am known for thinking of every eventuality. It is my profession."

Barney looked at Laura in horror and mouthed the single word, "Tonight!"

"Before we finalise details," the brigadier continued, "can I just congratulate Geoff on his swift handling of a potential threat. As you have doubtless seen in today's newspaper, he effectively dispatched the MI5 lad seen spying at my labs. Despite that blasted Barney boy still being a thorn under my skin, all is going like clockwork."

"Well, you know my views on that matter." The oily voice sounded annoyed.

"Yes, Geoff. I know Barney Jones was my idea." Jan's words were slurred but it was clear she was aggravated. "Don't go on about him again. OK, so I thought we could use him then get rid of him easily, that's all. I was wrong but it's no big deal. Anyway, he's on the run and he's no threat to us."

"Thank you, Jan," the brigadier butted in. "We've already discussed your string of errors with that Barney child. In hindsight, the wretched boy may not have been the best choice but he need not concern us now. Although he's taken longer to dispense with than envisaged, fear not. He is doubtless in police custody as we speak, hopefully being charged with murder and any tales about us will be totally ignored. Not that he will know anything. Should he be released on bail, Geoff will be waiting for him with a bullet or lethal injection. That child is history."

Barney frowned and pressed his ear to the phone, trying to listen through a burst of crackles. He smothered it under a pillow and whispered, "I just hope my phone isn't crackling down there and giving us away. I don't fancy either bullets or lethal injections."

The brigadier continued: "Talking of syringes, each of you should have received a few spare shots of smallpox vaccine for your nearest and dearest. You've obviously all taken your own doses in advance in order to be protected in time for tonight's spectacular release of the variola virus." He cleared his throat and spoke more softly. "I have now looked through this memory stick that Geoff took from the MI5 boy. It seems the lad had gathered a significant amount of evidence about us but failed to pass it on before Geoff wisely struck. I need to check some of the finer details on here to make sure none of his information was gleaned from an informer at the laboratories. Then I will destroy this to ensure our tracks will be covered. I am also issuing you all with these mobile phones for communicating tonight only. Afterwards they must be destroyed so that no police or MI5 forensics can trace our details or movements. You have a list of our numbers that you must subsequently destroy. One of these phones will be used to detonate the bomb but only I know that number. After all, we wouldn't want it to be triggered unintentionally at the wrong time. That's why I employed our explosives expert here to assemble it safely after this meeting."

Laura mouthed to Barney, "Bomb!"

"As you all know," the brigadier went on, "tonight's mission is a double-whammy. I'm killing two birds with one stone. I worked out this meticulous plan while I was languishing in prison. It can't fail. In addition to releasing the Speckled Monster fireworks, I intend to strike my old regiment and settle old scores. It's a matter of personal revenge. After the military band has performed at the

Tattoo and they're heading for home, their coach will explode with all on board, while heading south on the motorway. Any comments?"

"All's in order." Squint-Eye was talking now.

Barney recognised the voice instantly. He mouthed, "That's the squinty guy who threw me off the gallery at the Albert Hall."

"Once the Tattoo starts," Squint-Eye continued, "I'll load the coach with TATP packed in instrument cases. These won't be detected by sniffer-dog patrols, as proved by our previous research using that kid who's since become such a pain. The last dog patrol is twenty-two fifteen hours, when the bandsmen will be in hospitality. At twenty-two forty-five, Philippa will deliver the detonator bomb to the coach park. I will assemble this very soon using this mobile phone and Semtex. As sniffer dogs can detect this, Philippa will attach it at the last minute. It's in a magnetic box that will simply fix under the fuel tank. It can only be detonated by the mobile phone trigger. With all that TATP inside the luggage hold, the coach will be blown to oblivion. Your old regiment band, Brigadier, will be decimated."

"Excellent." The brigadier took a slow sip of water. "You and Geoff will be on the castle ramparts dressed as fireworks officials, ready to release our Speckled Monsters at twenty-two hundred hours. Meanwhile, from the top of Salisbury Crags at Arthur's Seat, Jan will be releasing the first attack to ensure maximum coverage of the east of the city, as well as being a back-up strategy, should the major assault be jeopardised, which, of course, it won't be. As you know, my meticulous military approach employs both belt and braces to ensure one hundred per cent success."

There was a long pause before a whispered question. "What about the money?"

The brigadier responded curtly. "Ah yes, I wondered when you'd get round to pay day, Geoff. Fear not, all is in hand. Each of you will receive your generous fees plus bonuses at midnight tonight at a little party in Geoff's apartment. I look forward to seeing you all then. But, at the moment—"

The phone crackled and died, but Barney had already heard enough. He switched it off and paced around the room. "There's no way they're going to get away with this. We've got to act fast, Laura, even though our chances are almost nil. We can't even use our phones now. But I still need to get hold of that memory stick. It's the only thing that's going to make anyone help us. If only I could get in room forty-two right now without being seen. Or maybe I can rush in, grab the stick and get out again before they can stop me. It might be worth the risk."

"Don't be absurd, Barney. You'd never be quick enough. But I could do it. They've never seen me before. I could dress up as a room maid or something."

"Are you mad? Don't even think about it."

"It's worth a try. I saw some cleaners' overalls in the cleaning cupboard downstairs. Leave it with me, Barney. I'll get that memory stick. You worry about other things."

Barney continued pacing up and down. "It's down to me to stop the fireworks going off – from two places at once. Impossible." He pushed his hands in his pockets as he paced, deep in thought, before pulling out the postcard Laura had given him in the church. He glanced at the picture briefly before returning it to his pocket. Suddenly he froze. "Oh blimey, that's just given me a crazy idea…"

He looked at his watch. "I haven't got long so I'll have to get going now. I'll meet you back in your room at the church hall some time after half-past ten, straight after I've done what I've got to do. In the meantime, you try to get that memory stick. Then you must do something to stop the soldiers getting on the coach after tonight's Tattoo. It's just possible we can beat them. Best of luck, Laura. I've got to dash…"

He ran out to the lift, leaving Laura sitting on the bed making sense of his gabbled instructions. "OK, then. Good luck," she said to the empty doorway. "So all I have to do is search the storeroom for an overall."

She knew only too well that her acting skills were about to be put to the test like never before. This was no comic show to delight the public, but a performance with far more serious consequences: a simple matter of life or death.

CHAPTER 29

Laura tapped on the door of room 42. She was dressed in a pink overall, holding a tray of cups and biscuits that she'd found in room 319. Slowly opening the door, she stepped inside and spoke in the East European accent she'd been rehearsing. "Sorry to disturb but you like the coffee?"

"I gave strict instructions we were not to be disturbed," the brigadier barked.

"I very sorry. I not hear message."

"You can leave those biscuits," Australia Head called to her.

"I put on table for you, yes?" She saw a memory stick on a red strap between two phones by the brigadier's glass.

"It's gone seven o'clock. I need to get to work." The man with the squint gathered up his notes, map and phone. "We need to be at our positions before nine."

A cup slipped off the tray, clattered across the table and knocked over a glass. Water sloshed on the brigadier's papers. "I so sorry," Laura cried. "I so sorry."

Hands grabbed at papers, glasses and cups, while the brigadier dabbed at the water with a napkin. "Just leave us. Go!" he barked.

"I so sorry," she repeated, backing her way out of the door. When she was in the corridor, she looked down in her hand and smiled. She slipped the memory stick into

212

her pocket. No one had seen her swap over two of the phones in all the commotion, either. Suddenly the door flew open and a hand grabbed her, pulling her violently back into the room.

"You're going nowhere, young lady."

The door slammed as she was pushed into a chair with her arms seized and pulled behind her, while another hand smothered her mouth. She had no time to scream.

"You're no Polish waitress. It took me a few seconds to remember, but I know just who you are now." Jan shouted a torrent of insults, her eyes wild with rage. "I recognise you from your school show. I came to see it – not by choice, I assure you. I was checking out that boy. But you were in it, too, weren't you? Admit it." She grabbed at Laura's hair and swore.

"Let us retain some dignity," the brigadier said, taking instant control. "If you are right, Jan, this girl will be dealt with swiftly. What do you have to say for yourself, young lady?"

Laura wasn't going to give up without trying. "I so sorry," she repeated, triggering another furious outburst of ranting. This time the woman with the eyebrow ring was screaming incoherently.

"Keep control, you fool." The brigadier threw water into Jan's face. "Get a grip of yourself. Leave this girl to me. I'll deal with her later in the apartment. You have syringes up there, Geoff?"

"Yes. But get rid of her body before we all get back. We don't want her spoiling the champagne reception." He took a roll of tape from his bag. "This'll shut her up."

He slapped a strip on Laura's mouth then wound

213

lengths of it round her wrists and ankles. She didn't struggle. Staying calm, she hoped, might stop the mad woman striking her. Despite her terror at the sight of such callous faces in front of her, Laura tried to switch off all emotion and concentrate on her acting. For the first time her audience was far from appreciative.

Philippa leaned forward and spoke softly. "So you must be a friend of the famous Barney. He obviously knows more than we thought. How many more of you has he told?" Laura could only shake her head.

Geoff looked at his watch and mumbled, "We haven't got time to question her now. It needs to be done properly back at the flat where she can scream as much as she likes. I need to get going. It's time to set up the fireworks."

He left the room, followed by the quiet man with a squint. The brigadier turned to the two remaining women, one of whom was muttering unintelligibly.

"Calm down, Jan. You have the Speckled Monsters in the car boot?"

"I told you. They're all ready."

"Good. Make sure you drink a few black coffees and calm yourself down before you drive over to Salisbury Crags in precisely…" He checked his watch. "Precisely six minutes fourteen seconds."

Jan shrieked, "I *am* calm! I'm perfectly OK. This kid has just freaked me, that's all. That blasted Barney keeps coming back to haunt me. I want to know what she was doing coming in here like that. Hold on, where's that memory stick? Quick, search her."

Philippa took from Laura's overall pocket a duster,

a handful of teabags – and the memory stick on a red strap. "There's more to this little madam than meets the eye."

"I knew it!" Jan wailed, her eyes wide and treacherous.

The brigadier stepped between them and seized the memory stick. "I'll take charge of this." He wound the strap and carefully placed it in his inside jacket pocket. "Well done on spotting this little fraud, Jan. But please, keep calm. I will deal with this while you focus on your duties. Gather yourself together and do your job well. I'll see you at midnight. Good luck."

Jan glared manically at Laura one last time before turning to leave the room. The door closed behind her as the brigadier bent down to put his mouth close to Laura's ear.

"She would have ripped you apart if I hadn't stopped her. So that's a very big favour you owe me. All I want from you is the truth. Everything. I get very touchy when my meticulous planning gets a glimpse of any little spanner in the works. But you will have no effect on our plans now. However, as I will need to extract certain information from you, it has suddenly become necessary to adjust my own itinerary to allow time for a period of interrogation. That's my speciality, I'm afraid. Brutal but effective. Then I'll inject you and dispose of your corpse in the canal."

He turned to smile at Philippa. "My dear, can you deliver this girl to the apartment within an hour?"

She smiled and proudly consulted her watch. "Easily. I'll fetch a large suitcase to shove her into, then load her into the boot of my car. No problem."

Laura blinked up at the two faces staring back at her.

She had no doubt she was in for a rough ride.

CHAPTER 30

The streets were full of noisy crowds in party mood, blissfully ignorant of the impending danger. As Barney ran past lines of parked coaches and darted between the milling revellers, he could hear the bands and bagpipes from inside the castle. The already darkening sky flashed with laser beams and spotlights from the ramparts, where officials were preparing for the great firework display. Two men in fluorescent jackets marked 'STAFF' had just joined them, with their boxes full of deadly rockets. One of the men had just assembled a bomb and placed it in the boot of Philippa's car, ready for her to deliver later. He'd expertly connected a mobile phone as the trigger mechanism and packed it with plastic explosives.

Barney's feet pounded on, his pulsing adrenaline flushing out all common sense – for he knew his plan was outrageous. He ran past the Demarco Roxy Art House displaying a poster emblazoned with 'Tonight's Show Cancelled', and on to the Pleasance Courtyard. Scurrying down familiar passages, he came to the doorway and stairs of last night's horror. In the corridor he stopped dead in his tracks. What a fool he was. As if everything would be back to normal and accessible for anyone to drop by. The stairway was taped off with 'Crime Scene' markers and 'No Entry' signs. Down the passage, a police officer with a clipboard was asking questions to passers-by. Although still wearing the wig, Barney felt sure he'd be recognised so he turned on his heels and ran back the way he came, his mind hatching another bizarre plot. It was a night for mad ideas so one more, he thought, wouldn't make much difference.

The scaffolding around the courtyard, displaying banners and strung with coloured lights, was easy to climb. Such was the relaxed mood of the crowd that no one seemed to notice or bother about a boy clambering through an upstairs window. No blanket hung over the glass now and floodlight spilled in from outside. Crouching on the floorboards, Barney stared at the mattress and solitary kettle of Seb's shadowy room. It was just as he'd left it, apart from a dusting of powder, presumably left by fingerprint investigators. The blue nylon bag, taller than himself, was propped in the corner and had also been dusted. The police may well have assumed it to be a tent bag, full of ropes and tent poles. Barney knew differently and it was this for which he'd risked returning.

Not seeing the kettle flex plugged into the wall, Barney caught his foot on it and the kettle tipped over with a clatter. Suddenly a key clicked in the lock and the door handle turned. Barney quickly grabbed the hang-glider and was back out through the window in seconds. Sliding down the scaffolding, with the cumbersome bag almost throttling him, he heard shouts of 'Stop that boy!" from the window he'd just clambered through. He didn't look back but slipped into the shadows and disappeared among the cheery crowd.

By the time Barney's sat nav had steered him through bustling streets, past junctions and along roads lit with takeaway signs, the sky was growing darker. So was the crag looming above him when he eventually reached open space and an almost empty car park. He ran over a zebra crossing to a footpath snaking uphill into the darkness beyond a signpost pointing to Arthur's Seat. According to his watch, it was already past nine o'clock. With the bulky bag pulling on his shoulder, he trudged awkwardly up the steep path winding all the way to the summit. He passed a few joggers and couples with dogs walking down from the top but otherwise all was strangely quiet after the hubbub of the city, now lighting up the sky behind him.

As he approached the summit, with a warm wind blowing in his face, Barney expected to see the woman with the eyebrow ring attending to her sinister duties. But there was no one – just heather rustling at his feet. He walked to the hilltop and looked over into a gully and across to the hill beyond. It was there he saw a lone stocky figure on the summit, a silhouette against the pink sky. If it was her, he was determined to stop her but he had no idea how, with time running out so fast.

Barney knelt in the long dry grass to unpack the hang-glider poles and battens, hoping he could work out how to assemble them in a hurry. Quickly locking the frame into place, stretching the fabric over the wings and fastening wires into what he hoped were the right places, he glanced down at his watch: 21.41. His heart began pounding at the thought of what he had to do in the next nineteen minutes. Standing with his feet on the very top of the hill, the bare rock dropping away in front of him, he remembered Seb's words: "Grip the control bar, leap off and throw back your legs into the harness." That inner voice gave Barney much-needed courage and he tried to imagine Seb spurring him on. "Just think you're a bird, that the wings are your own and the sky is all yours."

With a cry of "Geronimo!", Barney gripped the control bar, lifted the whole contraption above his head, ran into the wind and launched himself from the summit. The fear of his last crash dive returned in a wave of nausea, but as he pushed his feet further back into the harness, he felt the wings respond to his shift in balance and he soared effortlessly over the yawning drop below, gliding through silent emptiness towards the next rocky outcrop. Far ahead he saw the woman bending over a large cardboard box in a clump of gorse bushes, with a line of bottles beyond, at the cliff edge. These, he assumed, were how she planned to launch the deadly rockets over the east of the city, unless he could stop her.

Skimming over a straggle of prickly gorse, Barney released his legs from the harness in an attempt to land gently – but it had the opposite effect and he veered steeply, in a crash course with the woman, whose back was still turned to him. His silent approach took her so much by surprise that her scream was as much from shock as from rage. She fell into a thicket of thorns while Barney frantically scrambled from under the sprawled hang-glider, intending to grab the box of fireworks, but she beat him to it.

"Don't you dare take another step nearer!" she screamed. She grabbed one of the rockets and pointed it at his face. In her other hand she held a cigarette lighter.

"Don't think that stupid wig can fool me. I know who you are and before I blast you off the face of the earth, I'll tell you exactly what I think of you." She was screeching dementedly, her slurred curses spitting into the wind. Suddenly she stopped and, with foaming lips, snarled in a husky growl, " I wish I'd never set eyes on you. I thought you'd be the right kind of kid for us but you've been nothing but trouble. You've made me look a fool and they all laugh at me because of you. They call me the weakest link. And now you've had the nerve to come up here. Well, that was your second mistake. The first was to let your friend interfere. Unlucky – I saw through her act and she's about to be taken away and silenced forever."

"Laura? Where?"

"Never mind where. She'll be killed within an hour from now."

"Advocate's Close?"

The woman's eyes blazed, the dying light glinting in the pink quartz in her eyebrow ring. "Damn you! You think you know everything. You've been like grit in my shoe ever since I was mad enough to choose you at the airport. They warned me not to pick a kid and they were right. Finally, I can get rid of you once and for all." She flicked the cigarette lighter and a blue flame curled towards the fuse of the rocket still gripped in her hand, with its deadly test tube attached.

"Tonight hasn't come quick enough for me." She waved her arm wildly and the wind extinguished the flame. "In a couple of hours I'll get the money and I'll be gone. That's me out. I've hated this job, with all their sneering. That brigadier reckons he's so superior, always looking down his nose at me as if I'm scum. That's your fault. The others blame me for all the mistakes. Well I've had enough – do you hear?"

Barney edged nearer as her manic tirade continued, the madness flaming in her eyes more than ever. "It's all because of you. It was my idea to use you to test the sniffer dogs. I said you were the one we could use and train. But how was I to know you're a kid with attitude? You've been awkward from the start. Geoff never let me forget it. The brigadier has never stopped patronising me, every time you crop up with yet another problem. And as for her…"

Her rage flared like never before. "Korova indeed. She's the cow in all of this. All those expensive gifts he showers on his beloved Philippa. I get all the rough jobs while she swans about never getting her hands dirty and talking about me behind my back. I saw her face just now when your friend turned up. They all stared at me is if to say 'I told you so'. So that's why I detest you and why I'm going to light this rocket to slam in your smug little face." The lighter flashed again but Barney was ready this time. He sprang and knocked it from her hand as she lashed out with renewed fury. Flung against rocks, the lighter smashed, spraying lighter fuel across the dry grass, chased by a snake of purple flame crackling through tinder-dry scrub. Wind fanned the sparks into bushes which flared in a fierce blaze, spitting fiery splinters through the long grass in a pall of smoke that rolled across the hills, with angry flames racing and spiralling into the sky.

The woman was hysterical, screaming as she dived at the box packed with rockets, already belching out black smoke. "Heat will kill it! It'll destroy the virus."

The scorched cardboard buckled and suddenly erupted in a sheet of flames. Barney backed away at the searing heat and ran to the hang-glider. He had seconds to get away before the fireworks inside ignited. Although he felt sure the virus would instantly vaporise and die, the blast could be huge. He held the canopy above his head and ran into the wind, as thick smoke engulfed him. Suddenly the ground fell away beneath him and he tumbled off the edge of the crags. The hang-glider dipped and spun downwards before he could steady himself – just as a massive fireball ripped through the churning smoke behind him. When the thundering explosion was no more than an echo dying in the distance, the only sound was the woman's shrieks as flames poured from her clothes and she staggered blindly through the smoke before stumbling over the cliff and plummeting to the rocks below.

Choking and unable to see through stinging eyes, Barney swirled aimlessly, fearing he'd crash dive into the rock face. Swallowed by billowing black smoke and having lost all sense of direction, he grappled with the sat nav. He selected 'recent destination' and tapped 'castle'. Immediately the right-hand ring vibrated and he tugged on the control bar. The glider turned to the right and rose above the smoky cloud. Behind him, the fire rolled across the hilltop, coughing up more squalls of angry smoke, with the night sky glowing red beneath the stars.

Barney's pulse was racing furiously but not just from panic. He'd never witnessed anyone so scarily hysterical before and he hadn't meant to hurt her. That last image he'd glimpsed of her was sickening, and as he wrestled with thoughts of to how he could have saved her, a breeze filled the hang-glider's wings. He rose higher and the wind rushed exhilaratingly at his face as he looked down at the lights of the city moving far beneath him.

There was no time for Barney to dwell on the horrors of the last few minutes. His watch showed 21.54 and the castle was still a dark jagged outline ahead, rising high above the city rooftops. He'd need all his concentration to stay at the right height and on the right course. Too high and he'd sail over the castle into the flight path of shooting fireworks. Too low and he risked hitting spires and domes jutting above the roofs and chimneys – or even crashing into the castle walls in front of the cheering crowds. "Come on, Seb," he whispered. "Stay with me."

The hang-glider swept silently on, rising on thermals far above clock towers and huge cranes reaching across the sky, over streets swirling with lights where buses moved like toys beneath him. It soared over swaying treetops rustling in the darkness, and dipped almost low enough to touch a roof-garden wall. The wings banked and dipped at Barney's gentle tugs – or from any unintentional movement of his body. He was amazed at how clearly he could hear the sounds beneath him. When people looked up and waved, he heard every exclamation of surprise, until the drumming of marching military bands and the floodlit castle esplanade came into view. So did thousands of tiny heads in the audience and the cheering crowds on Castle Hill.

Shadowy figures with flaming torches moved on the castle ramparts ahead, behind a battery of cannons: the sign that the fireworks were about to begin. 21.59. Trying to steady the wings from a buffeting updraught, Barney aimed straight at a cannon in the hope of hovering just above it before landing on top of the battery – and before the first fireworks fired into him.

The castle towers seemed to be sweeping towards him faster than he intended. He slipped his feet from the harness and braced himself for impact against one of the turrets. It was then that he saw the man's horrified face squinting up at him. It was the same squinty-eyed man who'd thrown him from the gallery at the Albert Hall. Barney swooped over him, his foot swinging down and kicking him on the jaw. There was a roar of applause from the crowd at such a spectacular stunt, as the man fell backwards, disappearing from view inside the battlements. He grabbed up at Barney's legs and held on, but the wind dragged the hang-glider off the ramparts, lifting the two of them off the wall. Barney yanked on the control bar to turn the glider but the increased weight knocked it off balance and it swooped back again, just clearing the wall. Barney clattered inside the ramparts but the man clinging to his feet smashed into the muzzle of a cannon and fell like a stone. The crowd gasped as he bounced off the walls, dropped down the rock face and slammed onto railings in the street far below.

No sooner had Barney clambered to his feet and stood dazed on the battlements, than he faced Australia Head, snarling at him and waving a fire-torch. Behind him stretched a line of rockets the length of the wall, all waiting to be lit, with their test tubes still corked.

"Won't you ever give up?" the man spoke softly, coldly, dangerously. There seemed to be no emotion in his eyes at all. He lunged with the fire-torch. "There's no way I'm going to let you stop me. I've planned this for over a year. Tonight is pay-night. Do you really think I'm bothered by a scrawny little kid with an attitude problem? So say goodbye to this world. I've got a job to do."

This time the lunge was for real. The fire thrust into Barney's face. He saw it coming and twisted his body to dodge a direct hit. The flame roared by his ear and the torch hit the side of his head. He immediately smelt scorching as his hair caught alight. Except it wasn't his hair but the highly flammable wig. Tearing it off his head, he threw it into the face in front of him. The blazing hairball hit the man's chin, ignited his eyebrows and sent him staggering backwards. It gave Barney just enough time to grab a fire bucket full of water. The first slosh extinguished the fire-torch. The next drenched the row of waiting rockets.

"Once more I've put out the light," Barney said. "Like at our last fight in the storeroom."

The man was still dabbing at his eyes, but when he realised what Barney had done to the rockets, his mood changed. No longer the cool, emotionless professional, he became an enraged bull elephant. With his head down, he charged at Barney, who could only hit back with the bucket still in his hand. It cracked down on the man's head, on Australia itself, and it sent him reeling – just as a stirring crescendo rose from the bands in the arena below and the first fireworks from other ramparts ripped past them in a shower of bursting stars. Shocked at what he'd done, Barney lowered the bucket and stared as Australia Head staggered then lumbered towards him, grabbing the bucket and hurling it at Barney's face. Barney ducked and it flew over his head, clearing the wall and clattering into the security enclosure below. Heads looked up, astonished to see a man yelling obscenities and wrestling with a boy on the battlements – the boy clinging by his fingers, his legs dangling over the edge, the man lifting a hang-glider to slam down and hurl the boy out into the night.

Barney's fingers slipped on the slimy stone as the man stood over him, chewing and grinning. He raised the hang-glider victoriously above his head, ready to crash its nose into Barney's face. Heads in the crowd turned, fingers pointed and an officer ran to the steps leading up to the battlement.

With firm hands gripping the hang-glider bar, Australia Head swung his arms down at Barney's head, just as a gust of wind swept round the castle walls. The canopy lifted and the man's feet rose off the slabs. He hovered for a few seconds, just long enough for his grin to crack and for his chewing gum to stick in his throat. Just long enough for a screaming rocket shooting across the castle to strike the canopy in a sudden explosion and a fountain of golden shards. He clung on as the hang-glider swirled out into the sky in a burst of flashing blasts, before it flared up in a whirlwind of flames. It twisted, buckled and somersaulted before plunging through the night in a spiralling trail of sparkling green smoke. It slammed into the roof of a coach parked beneath the castle in a final shower of silver slivers. The man entwined in the twisted, buckled frame was dead before he hit the ground.

The band played on, almost drowned by the flutter of programme pages. Everyone wanted the name of the impressive choreographer for the spectacular Icarus display.

"What do you think you're doing, son?" The policeman's hand reached down, grabbed Barney's arm and hauled him up to safety. "That was a silly thing to do, don't you think?"

"Yeah." Barney was breathless and dazed.

"Don't you realise you could have hurt yourself coming up here? This is strictly off-limits."

"Yeah, it did cross my mind," he panted.

"The trouble with lads like you is that you don't consider the consequences of your foolish actions."

"Tell me about it!" Barney's laugh wasn't meant to offend.

"You kids just don't think about health and safety issues."

"I've been thinking of nothing else! Just make sure no one touches those rockets with the test tubes. That's smallpox in there, so get experts to make them safe."

The officer shone a torch into Barney's face. "Who are you? Hey, you look like the kid we're looking for…"

"That's right," Barney called over his shoulder as he ran to the top of the steps. "So you'd better come and get me. I'll be at Advocate's Close. Top apartment. And hurry."

He jumped and vanished into the smoky darkness.

CHAPTER 31

The brigadier looked out through the open window at popping speckles of colour peppering the night sky. "Spot on. Immaculate timing. J1 fireworks are underway!" He stood by a table set with candelabra, crystal glasses and an ice-bucket holding a bottle of champagne.

"In a week's time my vaccine will be selling like hot cakes. We'll be billionaires. But now, my dear, you must deliver the bomb. It's time for the next part of my infallible plan."

"Of course," Philippa said. "Shall I take the girl's body at the same time? I can easily drop her off in the canal."

"Shortly," he answered. "I want to get some information from her first. I'd rather you weren't here when I get her to squeal. It won't be pleasant. Since you found that memory stick on her, it's clear she knows too much. I'm experienced and I intend to get tough."

"I'm no shrinking violet, you know. I'm not squeamish."

"I just want to spare you the grisly side of this sordid business. My torture techniques aren't for your eyes. I like to think of you as being more sophisticated and civilised than the others. Jan is madder than ever, of course. I've got the chloroform ready for her tonight. I can't risk having her around any longer. Once she's unconscious, I'll finish her off with a lethal injection. The two men I'll keep until J2. Once they've finished the next attack in a couple of months at the Albert Hall, I'll make sure they meet up with a little accident. But I will protect you from all that, Philippa. You are the jewel in my crown."

He kissed her hand and caressed her watch. "And there will be plenty more exquisite jewellery for my favourite."

She laughed. "I'll just have one last word with the girl before I go." She walked into the bedroom, where Laura sat tied to a chair, the tape still across her mouth.

"I will give you one last chance to confess all before I go. The brigadier can be very brutal if left to his own devices. Tell me, where is your friend Barney and what is he up to? I have to say I had a soft spot for him. He's what I call sparky. This is your last chance to save yourself before things get very ugly." She peeled the tape from Laura's mouth.

The brigadier appeared at the door. "I wouldn't try to scream, if I were you. I can hit hard. You'll find out how hard very soon. I would advise you to answer my friend's questions truthfully if you don't want to suffer at my hands. She's so much gentler than me. I shall return in one minute when you need to depart, Philippa." He returned to the next room.

Laura blurted, "I expect Barney will be bringing the police here very soon." She tried to breathe calmly to stop herself panicking as she sensed the woman's false charm was a trick to make her talk.

"Wrong again," Philippa snapped impatiently. "Firstly, the police are after him and are hardly likely to listen to a word he says. Secondly, he doesn't know about here."

Laura took a gamble. "Barney's been here," she said. "That's how he knew about your meeting at the hotel. He found the agenda on a table."

The woman swore, pushed the tape back over Laura's mouth and returned to the other room. She and the brigadier were in deep discussion as a key turned in the lock.

Having dodged through police barriers and sprinted from the castle down the High Street, Barney had darted into the apartment block, up the flights of stairs and was now breathlessly pushing the front door open. He slowly sneaked along the hall towards the main room where he listened at the door. The brigadier was talking.

"The fool. I told Geoff to hide that agenda. But how did that kid get in here, for heaven's sake? It appears he's smarter than I thought."

"Don't worry," Philippa reassured him. "He'll never be able to out-wit you."

Barney turned and entered the bedroom. As soon as he saw Laura tied up in a chair, he crept over to release her and remove the tape from her mouth.

She smiled. "My knight in shining armour at last."

He brushed the hair from her eyes. "Am I glad to see you're safe! Don't worry, I'll get you out of here. I stopped the fireworks but we've still got to stop the bomb. That coach of soldiers will be leaving in about twenty minutes." He looked at his watch. "I've set my alarm. I'm determined to get all this sorted by the time it goes off. I reckon we've just got a few minutes to—"

A shadow appeared at his shoulder. "You've got time to do nothing… except die."

The brigadier stared down at them with cold, calculating eyes. "The sprat has caught the mackerel, it seems. Master Jones, I presume. We meet at last. A perfect end to a perfect day. How careless of you to steal the key and break in. Most unwise."

Barney's eyes darted around the room. The woman stood at the doorway, barring any means of escape. He knew the window led to certain death. There was no way out.

"Don't even think about it." The brigadier stepped forward and grabbed Barney's hair with one hand. He pulled his head back, swiftly took a neatly ironed handkerchief from his pocket and pushed it over Barney's face. Laura shouted until the woman slapped the tape back over her mouth and retied her wrists. Barney struggled for a few seconds before slumping on the floor.

"The chloroform was meant for you, my dear." The brigadier spoke softly in Laura's ear. "But there's still time. I find it makes the lethal injection so much calmer." He turned to the woman. "Tie the boy up and tape his mouth. He'll come round in a few minutes. I shall enjoy interrogating this irritating thorn in my side – before I remove it forever."

When Barney opened his eyes, he was aware of only two sensations as the room swirled around him. One was the tightness of the tape around his wrists and ankles; the other was music, interrupted by the brigadier's aristocratic voice.

"I always find a little Mozart makes for a more satisfactory euthanasia experience. This CD is most apt – 'The Requiem Mass in D minor'. Such a dignified herald of death."

The woman stooped to look into Barney's heavy eyes. "It's such a shame we can't have a little chat. I have to go and complete an assignment. By the time I return, I'm afraid you'll be at peace at the bottom of the canal. I just wanted to say goodbye."

"Au revoir," he grunted, as he tried to focus on her face and remember who she was. Her perfume soon told him. Elaine, the air hostess. The anger returned and he murmured, "Enjoy your prison sentence."

"Wrong again." She smiled patronisingly. "You've always been wrong. That was our mistake in choosing you. I've always believed you're no threat to us. I still think you're pretty harmless, just a pain now and again. I even thought you were quite cute, at first, with those lovely spaniel eyes. But even cute spaniels have to be put to sleep sometimes."

"The police are on their way." It was the only thing he could think to say. It sounded corny but he didn't care; he just wanted to sleep.

"Of course." She laughed. "That's the oldest bluff in the book. If only we'd kidnapped you in the first place, as I'd intended. Then we could have trained you properly. The girl who I snatched from the airport before you was a right little madam. She bit my hand and left a nasty flesh wound and now this ugly scar – so I had to dispose of her off Erskine Bridge. You were second choice but sadly you've turned out to be quite a disappointment. Never work with little brats."

As the anger rose inside him again, Barney blurted, "You're all finished. I've already got rid of your friends. I stopped the Speckled Monsters going off. It's all over."

"It certainly is for you. Sweet dreams…" She turned and took her car keys from her bag, where Barney glimpsed her tartan notebook. "You might be a good actress," he called after her. "You might play many parts – but they know the real you. The security services know exactly who you are. They've got your DNA."

She swung round on him. "Rubbish. I'm anonymous. That's my skill. I'm a chameleon, the mistress of disguise."

Barney smiled. "Mistress, possibly. Disguise, not really. I found your lip print and saliva on a plastic cup at the airport. You missed the bin when you threw it. Remember? MI5 were very grateful."

She glared, unable to speak, as Barney calmly added the final insult. "Your many voices and disguises aren't very convincing when you make the mistake of wearing that watch and always using the same tartan notebook. A bit of a giveaway, I reckon. So you're not as professional as you like to think."

She raised her hand and shrieked, "Kill him!" She slapped him hard across the face, then stormed from the apartment to drive the detonator bomb to its target.

Barney screwed up his eyes. "Blimey, that's helped wake me up!"

The brigadier scowled, adjusted his cufflinks and sat on the bed.

"You're worse than I thought. No one upsets her and gets away with it. I shall waste no more time." He opened a small attaché case and carefully lifted out a syringe.

"But time is now your biggest problem," Barney said coolly.

"Don't tell me about time," he bawled. "Time has always been my master. It is the key to successful strategy. Time is—"

"Nature's way of stopping everything happening at once."

"Shut up with your pathetic schoolboy humour. No one lectures me about time."

Barney tried to move his wrists to get a glimpse of the time and his watch-alarm. He wriggled his arms as the brigadier carefully examined the syringe. Barney's wrists were taped just above his watch and he was eventually able to twist the strap off. His watch dropped to the carpet without a sound, just as the brigadier delicately removed a plastic sheath from the needle, held the syringe up to the light and pushed out a fine spray from the shiny point. Barney kicked the watch across the room to the doorway.

"Would that be smallpox in the syringe, by any chance?"

The brigadier sneered. "You see, you know so little. That's state education for you. The variola virus is spread through the air. It must be inhaled and ingested. Whereas this syringe is a lethal dose of morphine. But you'll both be in the canal before it kills you. That way it looks like drowning under the influence of drugs. So much simpler for the coroner and all concerned. No messy murder enquiry. Death by misadventure."

"Just one question." Barney was desperately playing for time. "How did you get hold of the smallpox virus in the first place? I thought it was extinct."

"No longer." The brigadier glanced out of the window smugly. "It's now out there again – just released and fully alive. Only two storage sites were allowed to keep the last surviving frozen samples of the virus. One of these is in Russia. But with my Korova contacts, I was able, at last, to smuggle out just one drop containing the deadly organism. From that single culture, my scientists have developed litres of the lethal virus, as well as the money-making vaccine. Simple."

"You've got to be mentally deranged to come up with an idea like that."

"Or a genius." The brigadier sneered condescendingly. "But you wouldn't know about such things. You're obviously not well-educated and don't read much. Reading illuminates the mind. When I was your age, I read a story called *The Stolen Bacillus* by the masterful H. G. Wells. The bacillus, or germ, in question was a test tube of cholera bacteria, but that story inspired me to become a bio-terrorist. So you can blame literature for my wicked ways." He gave no hint of a smile.

"Maybe you were just born wicked. Books and Mozart may have stopped you being even worse," Barney continued, in the hope of keeping him talking. "But I can tell you certainly weren't born a genius, just a pathetic loser. You see, I've already beaten you. I've just ruined your entire stupid operation. It's over. Failed."

The brigadier snarled as a fleck of spit flew from his lip. "I am a noted military tactician. A professional to the core. It is impossible for someone of my calibre to be outflanked by a mere schoolboy. A scruffy tyke, at that – from a rather downmarket housing estate by all accounts. So *stop* these pointless delaying tactics." The word 'stop' sounded more like a sergeant major shouting orders across a yard, until it was drowned by Mozart's rousing crescendo.

The needle, with a single droplet glinting on its silver tip, moved towards Barney's arm. The brigadier lifted the sleeve. "Of course, I could just slam it into your body anywhere, but my training keeps me professional to the bitter end."

With one hand, he pinched the skin into a ridge on Barney's arm, before piercing it with the needle. He stared icily over his half-rimmed spectacles. "It's no use you trying to wriggle. You can't stop me now." A single bead of blood rose and trickled from the tiny pinprick in Barney's arm. As the music faded, the brigadier raised his thumb to press down the syringe – just as a sudden squawk filled the room. Startled, the brigadier turned. The shriek at the doorway reverberated around the apartment. A crowing cockerel. The rooster alarm watch.

In the second the brigadier looked away, Barney struck. He kicked up with both feet, and with all the force he had left. The blow threw his chair backwards with him still tied in it. Laura could only watch helplessly as he crashed beside her.

The strike on the brigadier's chin threw him against

the wall with a crack to his head. He fell, sprawling across the carpet with a grunt and smacking his jaw on the skirting board. He groaned and lay still on his back before convulsing. Slowly he rolled over, his face twitching and his arms shaking in spasms, before he scrambled to his hands and knees to crawl drunkenly to the bed. As he pulled himself to his feet, the rooster alarm finally stopped. The following seconds felt like an eternity. Barney could only lie and watch as the brigadier, seething with anger, regained control and staggered forwards. The music returned with a dramatic chorus.

Nobody moved until the brigadier swayed and looked down, eyes burning with rage and horror. His shaking hand reached down slowly to pull the syringe from his leg. The needle had stabbed firmly in the back of his knee. He wrenched it out with a throaty growl and threw the empty syringe to the floor. His brow was sweating and all colour drained from his face as he mumbled, "Ph-Ph-Philippa. Help me. Come back." He stumbled to the bedside phone where his shaky fingers fumbled over the number pad.

Had the tape not been stuck across her mouth, Laura could have given a warning. When she'd swapped the two mobile phones at the hotel, she had seen who'd picked them up. The man who left to assemble the bomb had taken the woman's phone to fix as the trigger device. It was the phone whose number the brigadier was slowly pressing with trembling fingers. He hardly had time to lift his finger from the final digit when the whole room shook and a blinding white flash shuddered at the window, followed by a booming thud and the distant sound of shattering glass.

The brigadier croaked feebly into the phone. "Ph-Phili-Philippa."

Laura watched him dab his face and loosen his collar as he stood up shakily, unsteady on his feet, then lurch from the room holding onto a chair, then the doorway for support. His throat gurgled as he began whimpering pitifully. Barney heard him stumbling into the next room, then crash into the table, knocking the ice bucket to the floor in a shower of ice cubes and shattering glass. Neither of them saw the desolate look on his grey contorted face as he peered down from the open window to the flames pouring from the twisted wreckage of Philippa's car. Nor did they hear his cry as he slouched onto the balcony and slumped over the rail. He fell silently through the rising black smoke to the street far below.

The first police car roared to a halt, siren blasting, just metres from the blazing car. It was too late to save the woman slouched over the steering wheel engulfed in flames. Minutes later, an officer saw what she thought was a rubbish sack hanging on the fence for collection next morning – now lit by flames and flashing blue light. It turned out to be a brigadier, impaled on the railings' sharp iron spikes.

Barney and Laura struggled to free themselves but the tape held. The last stirring chords of Mozart's 'Requiem' finally echoed around the apartment, just as armed police burst through the door and froze in the haunting stillness.

CHAPTER 32

The interview room at the police station had pale green walls and an electric clock that was ten minutes slow and buzzed annoyingly.

"You'll be delighted to hear, young man, that the charges against you have been dropped and we've been able to confirm that much of what you've told us is spot-on." The police officer put a plate of biscuits on the table in front of Barney. "Help yourself, son – seeing as you're not the nasty little thug we thought you were."

"Does that mean I'm free to go?" Barney bit eagerly into a custard cream.

"Of course. However, it would be very nice if you could stay on for a while to help us with some of the finer details. Besides, your father will be here soon. I've had a long chat with him explaining your exploits and how you've given us a mountain of paperwork for a Sunday afternoon." The officer winked. "Have as many biscuits as you want."

"I thought I'd told you everything several times already. I'm worn out!" Barney looked at his watch. "I need to get back for this afternoon's show."

"Relax," the officer said. "It's your day off. When your teacher was here earlier she told me there's no show today. Mind you, she gave me strict instructions to let her know when you'll be back."

Barney laughed. "That was Mrs Peters. I'm glad she doesn't work for the police. She didn't believe a word I told her about what's been happening. I'm sure she still thinks I've made up all this stuff. Now Laura's gone back with her, she might listen to the full story and actually believe me."

A woman officer entered the room, clutching a bundle of papers. "Talk about keeping me busy, Barney. I've been on the phone all morning."

He looked up anxiously. "So what about the test tubes of smallpox? Are they safe and have you found the memory stick? It was on a red strap. It must be in the flat somewhere."

Her smile reassured him. "Fear not. Some of the best scientists this city has to offer are dealing with those test tubes as we speak. All the fireworks have been made safe. None of the virus, I'm pleased to report, has escaped. One of our IT specialists is also at work downloading information from the memory stick recovered from the deceased gentleman's pocket – the one referred to as the brigadier. The Ministry of Intelligence is already on the case."

"Does that mean Aries knows about all this now?" Barney asked.

"Possibly. I certainly think you're being discussed at a senior level. It seems you're quite famous, judging by all the phone calls we're getting."

"I've probably got a few messages from Mum on my phone. The trouble is, it's still in the ceiling of room forty-two at the Clarence Hotel."

"It's all in hand," the woman said cheerfully. "One of our community officers is already over there fetching it. We've been trying to contact your mother but haven't been successful yet."

There was a knock at the door and a man's head appeared. "There's a Mr Jones here to speak to the boy. Shall I send him in?"

The woman looked at Barney. "Are you all right with that? We'll leave you to chat with your dad unless you'd like one of us to stay."

Barney nodded. "Yeah, that's fine. I'll scream if he turns violent!"

The officers left the room and Barney's dad bustled in. "Barney, are you OK? I've just been hearing about what you've done. I had no idea…" He put his hand on Barney's shoulder. "You must be totally shattered."

"Yeah, Dad, I am. It's all a bit unreal. Thanks for coming over. Sorry about all the hassle and disturbing your Sunday lie-in."

"I'm so relieved you're OK. When they called yesterday and told me you'd killed a guy and were on the run, you can imagine what it's been like. Gran said it was obviously all rubbish but…"

Barney chuckled. "But you weren't so sure! Good old Gran. I'm glad she's got faith in me. How is she, Dad?"

"She's… well, she's… yeah."

Barney looked worried. "There's something wrong, isn't there? There's something you don't want to tell me."

"Before I tell you," he fetched a chair and sat beside him, "I just want to say something to you." Placing his hands on Barney's shoulders, he looked him in the eyes. "Listen, Barney – what you've done and what you've gone through is absolutely amazing. I never realised…" His voice cracked and he struggled to speak. Clearing his throat and taking another breath, he continued slowly, "I never appreciated before what a great kid you are. Seriously, Barney, I'm so proud of you. Well done, son."

Barney threw his arms around him. "You've never said anything like that before. Thanks, Dad. We don't normally do hugs, do we? I just wish I could share this moment with Gran. Please tell me, Dad. Is it bad news about her?"

His dad took out his phone and pressed a key. "Well, it's like this, Barney – there's something you need to know."

"What is it? Is she in hospital?"

"No, Barney. She's out in the car and she's just coming in to see you. She's fine!"

Barney waved his arms and cheered. "Just wait till I tell her what I've been up to."

"She's over the moon with you. I couldn't stop her coming to see you. We're both gob-smacked at your courage. The thing I'm so chuffed about is that you knew right from wrong. You weren't afraid to fight to do the right thing despite massive risks. I really admire you for that. You've always been a stubborn little blighter and a real daredevil!"

"With an attitude." Barney smirked before adding thoughtfully, "I've done a lot of thinking the last few days – about big stuff. Like life and death. I guess that changes you and how you look at things."

The door opened and a panting Labrador with thrashing tail leapt in. When Gran appeared, led in by an officer, she called excitedly, "Barney, come and give me a hug!"

"Gran, how are you? I've been worried about you."

"I'm fine. They've given me different tablets and I'm a new girl. I don't have to have the op now. But never mind about me, how did you do all those wonderful things I've been hearing about?"

"I can safely say you saved my life, Gran. At least, your sat nav did, as well as your rooster watch. And as for you, Melda…" He held the dog's head in his hands then patted her enthusiastically as the woman officer returned with Barney's phone.

"Here we are, young man. All recharged and all yours."

Barney's dad led Gran to a chair. "Have you spoken to Mum about all this, Barney?"

"No, she's away for the weekend with Owen. She's got other things on her mind, I guess. To be honest, I don't really want to ask about when they're getting married."

Gran leaned forward and held his hand firmly. "I think you ought to call her, love. We mothers worry when we don't hear from our sons."

Barney switched on his phone. "OK then, but I bet she won't answer."

He waited and listened. "I don't believe it – she's got it switched on."

After a long silence, he gave a thumbs up and said, "Hi, Mum. How's it going?"

"Hello, love. Are you having a good time?"

"Er, well, it's a long story. Have you seen the news today?"

"No, Barney – why?"

"I'll tell you later, Mum."

"Sorry if you've been trying to get hold of me. I switched off my phone for a while. We went on a very long walk. It's all been a bit heavy here."

"How's Owen?"

"I've got no idea."

"Mum, are you OK?"

"I've never felt better. Love, you were right. He was no good for me. We've had a long discussion and I decided to get rid of him and move on. Like you've always told me, he's not the brightest bulb in the pack."

"Did I say that? Sorry, Mum."

"I should have listened when you said he's only got two brain cells and one of those is on its last legs!"

"Did I say that, too? Mum, I'm sorry I've been such a pain lately."

"I've decided there's only one man in my life right now and it's you, Barney. I can't wait for you to come home. There's so much to talk about. Have you got much news, love?"

"Just a bit. I think you'll be impressed. So Mum, does that mean you don't want me to move away?"

"Whatever gave you that idea? Listen, Barney – I'm sorry I said all those things. I was a bit stressed, that's all. You'll understand what that means one day. You're a bit too young to know about panic attacks, life-changing decisions and that kind of thing."

"Yes, Mum. Maybe."

He laughed raucously, hugged the dog, jumped on a chair and punched the air. "Yes!"

CHAPTER 33

The night sky flashed and crackled with shuddering explosions of swirling colour. Crimson smoke drifted over the castle ramparts and shimmering rooftops.

"To this time next year!" Mrs Peters raised her glass.

Barney rested his arm on the balcony rail. "Surely you won't bring a show here again next year, miss. Not after all this palaver."

"I don't see why not. I may have a few more grey hairs as a result of all your shenanigans but it seems to have turned out rather well in the end. Tonight's final performance was the best yet. The show's even been nominated for *The Evening News* Best Production Award."

"In that case," Barney laughed, raising his bottle of coke, "to this time next year!"

"I think Mrs Rickman ought to get an award for best director," Laura said, "and Barney for Hero of the Year."

Barney moved towards the French windows leading back into the room set out for their party. "Can we go back and join everyone else now, miss?"

"Not yet," she answered curtly. "I asked you both out here for a reason. Someone wants a quick word with you."

Barney caught sight of a face through the glass. The eyes were watching – staring. Sharp, steely eyes were moving ever closer. The French window opened and out stepped Aries with a glass in her hand.

Barney couldn't stop himself, "Oh, crikey!"

Aries did not smile. "Although I never thought I would say this," she said after a long, slow sip of her martini, "I've heard from good authority that an award from Number Ten could well be on the cards. The Prime Minister is highly impressed with your efforts, it seems. Although I'm rarely impressed by anyone, I can safely say you've finally done it, young man."

He beamed. "Does that mean I'm forgiven for gouging your car with a hang-glider?"

For once she smiled. "There's something about you I've grown to tolerate, Barney. Let's face it, you were dead right about Korova and about them targeting the Royal Albert Hall in the following months. They were planning to do the next phase, J2, down in London at the Festival of Remembrance. Seb's memory stick has been invaluable in providing all kinds of leads. We certainly mopped up this case swiftly after your input. Seb's sacrifice wasn't for nothing, you'll be pleased to know."

"I wouldn't have done what I did without the thought of him spurring me on. Seb's voice was in my head all the way when I was trying to fly his hang-glider."

Aries glanced up at another spray of fireworks above the castle. "His death wouldn't be in vain if you decided to carry on in his footsteps."

Barney raised his eyebrows and opened his mouth in surpise. "Does that mean you'll be wanting my services again one day?"

"Undoubtedly. Unless it involves a hang-glider." Aries's smile didn't last. "In all seriousness, Barney, I'd like to talk to you at length back at HQ for a proper debrief. They've only just shown me how far you had to run and hang-glide the other night. However did you do it? You must have superhuman stamina. I don't know what you're on, but I wouldn't mind some of it!"

"Just adrenaline EPS."

"EPS?"

"Extra Panic Strength."

"Well it obviously works! By the way, Barney, I've got you a card – as one Aries to another. Seeing as I missed your birthday in April." She handed him an envelope. "They call me Aries because I'm Number One, the first in the zodiac year, but you are the genuine thing."

"I've never understood all that zodiac stuff," he said, as he opened the card showing a ram on the front.

"You will now," she said. "Just read the description. It's you in a nutshell."

Barney read it slowly:

**"Adventurous and energetic
Pioneering and courageous
Enthusiastic and confident
Dynamic and quick-witted
On the dark side...
Selfish and quick-tempered
Impulsive and impatient
Foolhardy and daredevil"**

He laughed as he read aloud the description on the back:

"Your immense energy makes you restless, argumentative, occasionally headstrong and capable of holding grudges. You like extremes: physical, emotional and mental – but if your extremism goes too far beyond social acceptability, then expect to be extremely lonely."

Mrs Peters nodded. "No comment."

"Fair play, miss." He chuckled. "I can't really argue with this. But what about the MI5 Aries – how many marks out of ten would you give me for being… foolhardy and a daredevil?"

Aries cast him one of her withering stares. "It grieves me to admit this but, all in all, I'd award you an A plus."

"Wow. Did you hear that, Mrs Peters? An A plus. Would that be A for Aries or Attitude, by any chance?"

Mrs Peters bristled. "Let's not go there," she said. "Instead, I think we'll go indoors for supper and join everyone else. We'll avoid the 'A' word and enjoy a good party."

She led the way through the French windows, to the awaiting buffet.

Barney was about to follow when Laura held his arm. "So what's the secret of your success?" She giggled.

He turned to see her cheeky grin and glinting eyes. "I think you know the answer." Leaning back with both elbows on the balcony rail, he looked her fully in the face. "Thanks for everything. Especially this." He took a crumpled postcard from his pocket. "It was this picture of a massive eagle soaring in the sky that gave me the mad idea. I only looked at it properly when everything was over. It's what you gave me in that church when we were so tired and I was ready to give up. I reckon this card stopped me nose-diving out of the sky." He looked again at the outstretched eagle's wings and the text printed below:

Isaiah 40, verse 31:
Those who trust in the Lord will find new strength.
They will soar high on wings like eagles.
They will run and not grow weary.

Laura laughed, "So it's my fault you jumped off a cliff, is it?"

"I guess this gave me confidence to soar high on wings. Mind you, I reckon I was more of a turkey than an eagle! It was a miracle I didn't crash dive this time."

"A miracle? I thought you said you weren't religious," she teased.

"I didn't think I was but I actually said three prayers in that church last week; one for Gran, one for Mum and one for us. It seems like they might have worked."

She leaned forward, closed her eyes and kissed him, as a final flurry of fireworks flew across the sky in a spray of splintering silver that burst over the city in a blinding blaze.

"Wow. Some kiss!" Barney's face flashed under a fizzing shower of stars, the final sparks flickering in Laura's shining eyes.

"Well, that's just the first. There's plenty more where that came from." She winked. "Thanks to you, of course."

"So it looks as if my improved attitude has impressed you, too." He grinned, resting an elbow back on the rail and thoughtfully peering down into the street where a hazy moon and dying splinters of silver shimmered over shiny cobbles.

"No doubt about it. I said a prayer in that church, too. It was for us – but probably I asked for something a bit different from yours. Something extra." She whispered softly in his ear and kissed him again… very slowly this time, as a final peppering of sparks above their heads dissolved forever into the serenely still and smoky night.

"Could smallpox really return? The complete absence of any cases for over 30 years can only mean that it has been annihilated from free existence on the planet and it is unlikely (but not beyond the bounds of possibility) that it could escape from the high security vaults in the CDC (Center for Disease Control in the USA) or Koltsovo (in Russia)."

From *'The Angel of Death'* – the story of smallpox by Gareth Williams (2010)